The Book of Blaise♥

♥ or *How to Survive the Menopause with your Manhood Intact*

First published in 2015 by Cloudberry Books
Text copyright © Ian Macpherson 2015

The moral right of Ian Macpherson to be identified as the author of this work has been asserted by him in accordance with the Copyright, Designs and Patents Act, 1988.

All rights reserved. No part of this publication may be reproduced or transmitted in any form by any means, electronic or mechanical, including photocopying, recording or any information storage or retrieval system, without either prior permission in writing from the publisher or by licence permitting restricted copying. In the United Kingdom such licences are issued by the Copyright Licensing Agency, 90 Tottenham Court Road, London W1P 0LP.

www.ianmacpherson.net

A CIP catalogue reference for this book is available from the British Library.

ISBN 978-0-9569056-1-1

Typeset by Freight in Plantin
Printed and bound by Bell and Bain, Glasgow

The Book of Blaise♥

Ian Macpherson

To Suzanne.

Fond memories of Words In Progress.

Ian

Oct 2015

♥ or *How to Survive the Menopause with your Manhood Intact*

For Magi

my one wish –
that we die together
at the age of 96
making love

with all our children

at the bedside

Contents

Dream Lover Two	1
A Brisk Hike Up The Trossachs	13
Soggy Bottom Baby	23
Death of a Ladle's Man	33
The Thing You Did Last Time	41
Fecund	55
War and the Menopause	65
Salmon Chamareemo	75
Are Women Funny?	83
Bottled Air	91
Occasions of Sin	101
You Have The Right To Remain Silent	111
Scrotum	127
The C Word	141
Twice a Catholic	171
Entwined	185

Bonus Stories

Prune Surprise	205
The Nut House	215
Round Ireland With An Inanimate Household Object	223
Acknowledgements	231

Dream Lover Two

In daylight I can always tell when Blaise is upset. The face gives it away. At 4.32am, however, I have to rely on vocal hints. Sobs. Suppressed sniffles. The rustle of yet another tissue being removed from its box. Often all three in that order. Sob, sniffle, rustle. Sob, sniffle, rustle and so on.

I mention this because it was now one of those 4.32s. Sob, sniffle, rustle. Before the next sob I placed my left arm on her pillow and she moved towards me, throbbing gently in her grief. I said nothing, contenting myself with giving her silent support. I like to think I'm good at this sort of thing. Masterful yet gentle. What's the word I'm looking for? Empathetic. So there she was and there was I.

Sobbing. Sniffling. Rustling.

Empathising.

Time passed. 4.33. Sob, sniffle, rustle. The silent empathy patently wasn't working.

'What's the matter?' I said.

'Nothing,' she whispered. So I went into my *there-there* routine. *There there. There there there.* She moved closer. Interesting how a man thinks of carnal desire at this point. I thought about it. Based on previous experience I suppressed the thought. *There there*, I continued. *There there there.*

'It's just,' she sobbed, 'I had a very upsetting dream.'

Now here I could help. I'm very big on dreams. 'I see,' I said. 'So what was it about?'

'Oh, nothing,' she sighed. 'It was – it was just a dream.'

'There there,' I said. Then I waited.

'I was asleep,' said Blaise.

'I know,' I said.

'No,' she said. 'I mean in the dream.'

'I see.' This was in danger of getting complicated.

'I woke up suddenly,' she said. 'Someone was throwing pebbles at the window.'

'That's modern life for you,' I sighed. 'Maybe we should move to the country. So, was *I* still asleep?'

'You weren't in it,' said Blaise. 'It wasn't that sort of dream.'

I was a bit taken aback by this matter-of-fact response. Still, it was her dream. Let her sort out the pebbles. I removed myself mentally from the dream bed.

'Go on,' I said, in my best dream-therapist's voice.

'It was a four-poster bed,' said Blaise. 'Sort of nineteenth century.'

I added four posts and adjusted the time frame but said nothing.

'I lit a candle,' she continued, 'and tiptoed to the window.'

Drama. Good.

'The moon was shining on a placid, melancholy ocean.'

I was having to work overtime on the visuals, but gave Blaise her head.

'A young man stood in the moon-kissed garden. Apple blossom everywhere. He was about to throw some more pebbles.'

I may have stiffened slightly.

'Young?' I said. 'How young?'

'I don't know. Sixteen?'

'Hardly a man, then,' I said. I was on high alert. A sixteen year old boy? I wasn't in it? Not that sort of dream? I didn't like the sound of this. That said, it's difficult to have a free and frank exchange of views with your arm in the *there-there* position. So I said nothing. Just brooded quietly. Blaise, on the other hand, seemed to relax into her narrative. Almost as if I wasn't there.

'He had the most beautiful soulful eyes,' she said. 'And a flop of dark hair that – oh, it was so poetic.' I need hardly add that I used to have the most beautiful soulful eyes. Not to mention a flop of dark hair that was oh et cetera. But there we are. I wasn't in the dream. I gave Blaise the metaphorical floor. 'I think he may have been consumptive,' she continued. Oh, *please*. Consumptive? I gave up. 'He said,' wept, yes, *wept* Blaise, 'he said he'd loved me before time and would love me after time.' I was tempted to ask about the bit in the middle, but Blaise wept on. 'He – he threatened to kill himself if I didn't return his love.'

Silence. I waited. Nothing. 'So *you* said?'

'That's when I woke up,' sniffled Blaise.

'So you said nothing.'

'Well,' she said, 'I might have said I'll think about it.'

And then – brace yourselves for this because I found it difficult to believe myself – Blaise fell into a deep, untroubled sleep. I, in contrast, lay awake for the rest of the night, my thoughts dark and malevolent, my arm stuck in the *there-bloody-there* position. Not that it mattered much. Due to a lack of circulation beyond the left shoulder, it died at 5.02.

Next day, Blaise, thanks to a long lie in, was all sweetness and smiles. I, on the other hand, festered. Nothing too obvious. More of a slow burn effect which brought out Blaise's maternal side. 'What's the matter?' she said.

'Oh, nothing.'

So she went into a female variation of the *there-there* treatment. The stroking of the hair. The comforting kiss on the cheek. The cuddle. Interesting how a man's thoughts turn to carnality at such moments. I know mine did. But I also continued to fester. My mind worked over the salient points of Blaise's dream. The soulful eyes and flop of hair. The consumption and the emotional blackmail, and then, to top it all off, '*I'll think about it.*'

The last bit must have popped out involuntarily. Blaise disengaged. 'Think about what?' she said. I reminded her of the denouement of her dream. 'Oh, *that*,' she said. 'I'd forgotten all about it.' I refreshed her memory. The bullet point version. 'Oh, *right*,' said Blaise. 'Poor boy. I mean, I was old enough to be his mother.'

'Perhaps,' I replied, not un-icily, 'that was the attraction.'

Blaise giggled involuntarily. 'You're not jealous, are you?'

'Don't change the subject,' I said. 'Certainly not. However, if you happen to meet the young reprobate again, tell him you're spoken for.'

'Meet him again?' Blaise spluttered. 'A dream is not a film! You can't just assemble the same cast and shoot part two.'

I lowered my eyebrows for effect.

'I did say *if*.'

'Well,' said Blaise, 'if by any chance we meet again I'll pass your message on. Happy?'

'I'm always happy,' I said darkly. 'It's my nature.'

Blaise's laughter suggested that she, at least, had made a full recovery; and there the matter rested. For then. I may have brought the subject up once or twice during the course of that evening. Dreams, after all, are pretty indicative of something or other to do with the subconscious. Example. I had a dream once in which my penis had turned into a cigar. One of those large Cuban ones, for those interested in such matters. Recently lit. I still have no idea what, if anything, the dream was trying to tell me. Having said that, I've always been secretly pleased it wasn't a Slim Panatella. But I digress.

The following morning I brought Blaise a cup of tea in bed. The rattle of the saucer may have woken her. Difficult to tell. But she opened her eyes like a startled sparrow. 'You again,' she yawned. To be fair, it wasn't the first cup of tea, but we won't go into that.

'Well?' I said.

'Well what?' Blaise sat up.

'Anything further on the dream front?'

'Nothing to report, I'm afraid. I expect they didn't get funding.' If this was a reference to the film version it was in pretty poor taste. I decided to let it pass.

'You're quite sure,' I said.

'Quite,' she said. 'And please don't stare like that. You look like Bible John.' I didn't know who Bible John was. Possibly a relative. But I caught my reflection in the wardrobe mirror and disliked him on sight. I smiled genially. Blaise studied me as she sipped her tea.

'Grimace,' she said. 'Lovely word. I must use it in a poem.' There was no point talking to her when she was in this sort of mood, so I decided to go about my business. I had just reached the door when she sighed softly into her cup.

'It was only a dream,' she said. 'Really.'

'Ah, but was it?' I said. I decided to leave it there, and was about to close the door for dramatic effect when she put her cup down on the bedside table.

'Hold on,' she said, placing her fingers to her temple. 'I'm getting something.'

'You are?'

'I *did* have a dream last night. Yes. It's all coming back to me.'

I closed the door and moved to the end of the bed. 'And?'

'Shhh.' Blaise was concentrating hard. 'He was in it. Yes. That's it. He came back. The boy. He came back the following night. More pebbles. Or did I just leave the window open and wait? Anyway, he came back, that's the important thing. Apparently the consumption had been a misdiagnosis. He just had a slight chest cold.'

This sounded like a real breakthrough. 'Go on.'

'Wait. It's coming. Yes. That's it. He'd decided to join a closed order of monks.'

'What? Like – Cistercians?'

'Could be. He didn't specify. Just said they were closed. Then – what was it he said then? Yes. That's it. He apologised for his little outburst the previous night. Said he'd been running a temperature.'

'Sounds like a very verbal dream,' I said.

'I'm a poet,' said Blaise. 'I work with words. It's bound to have an influence.' I supposed so. 'Anyway, we shook hands on that and promised not to keep in touch. You know, what with him being enclosed and everything.'

'You shook hands?' I said. 'I thought you were upstairs.'

Blaise may have looked startled. If she did she recovered quickly.

'It was a bungalow, silly. You know. One of those seaside towns. Probably Largs.' She patted my hand. 'So. Nothing to worry about. THE END.'

Hmn. It certainly had the ring of truth. I'd been to Largs off-season and anything was possible. I felt reassured. We had our old relationship back. Or so I thought. The following afternoon, however, I was forced to reassess. I'd just arrived back from a trip to the library[1]. Blaise was in the living room. She was in high spirits with person or persons unknown. I closed the front door softly and kept a low profile as I negotiated the hall.

'So *I* said *He's joined a closed order of monks*,' said Blaise, 'and that seemed to do the trick.'

'Brilliant,' said the voice of her best friend Faye, and they were both tinkling merrily when I opened the living room door.

'Not interrupting anything, I hope,' I said. 'Do carry on.'

They didn't. Faye stood up to give me a kiss on the cheek as if the world hadn't just shifted on its axis.

'So,' I said genially. 'What's all this about monks?'

I'll say this for them. They both had the good grace to freeze. Blaise recovered first. 'I see,' she said accusingly. 'You were listening in.'

'Not so,' I said. 'I'm afraid I had no control over the volume. Nor,' I continued wittily, 'did there appear to be

---

[1] *Sometimes a Penis is just a Penis: Dreams Demystified*. Well, it was a start.

an off switch.'

'Well, anyway – ' Blaise began, intending no doubt to bluff it out. Faye put a hand on her arm.

'No,' she said. 'He's right. We have an issue here.'

'We?' I said. '*We*?'

'We,' said Faye. 'After all, I'm not a Jungian analyst for nothing.'

I folded my arms meaningfully. 'Really?' I said. 'A Jungian analyst? Last time you were here I could have sworn you said you were a nutritionist.'

Faye waved nutritionist away. 'I *dabble* in nutrition,' she said. 'Strictly mealtimes. Jungian analysis is my *passion*. With a bit of that other one. You know.'

'Freud,' said Blaise helpfully. Was it my imagination or did Faye look genuinely relieved.

'That's the one,' she said. She lowered her voice. 'They didn't get on,' she confided, 'So I'm not, *strictly speaking*, allowed to say his name.'

'I was referring to Anna,' said Blaise. Faye looked blank for the merest hint of a nanosecond.

'Ah yes,' she said. 'Anna. Seminal. Quite, quite seminal.' She slipped her arm through mine. 'You know,' she said, as if Blaise was somehow excluded from the conversation, 'a quick session might be the very thing.'

'If anyone needs treatment,' I all but snorted, 'it should surely be the person who had the dream.'

Faye poked my ribcage in a very unladylike manner. 'Do you question my methods?' she said, dropping her voice, for some reason, to a male register.

'But won't it tire you out?' said Blaise. 'Faye has chronic fatigue syndrome,' she explained.

'Nonsense,' said Faye. 'I'll take the couch. Now scoot,'

she said, waving Blaise away. 'This is confidential.'

Blaise scooted. Faye settled herself on the sofa, while I sat on a straight-backed wooden chair and awaited further instructions.

'So what's the procedure?' I asked. Faye seemed momentarily thrown by the question.

'Tell me everything,' she said. 'Leave nothing out.'

'You mean – ' I began.

Faye put her hands behind her head and prised her shoes off with her feet.

'Exactly,' she said. 'Absotootley.'

I had a certain understanding of the procedure, mainly gleaned from New York Jewish cinema and, indeed, the New York Jewish novel. Not to mention the odd short story, TV series or play. Also New York Jewish. So I began at the beginning. Bit of prehistory for contextualisation purposes. Birth. Early years. Education, trauma of. Failure to observe Hanukkah because both my parents were goyim.

Throughout all of this Faye lay still, eyes shut, her face a mask of total concentration. I'd sailed through my early years with aplomb and was about to enter the choppy waters of adolescence when I noticed that Faye's breathing had become regular and potentially intrusive. I coughed politely. She sat up with a how-the-hell-did-I-get-here look.

'I take it you missed all that,' I said. Meaningfully.

'Pas du tout,' she said. 'It's how I work. Why do you think they call it dream analysis?' She wiped the sleep from her eyes. 'But do go on.'

'Where was I?' I asked. Rhetorically as I thought.

'Masturbation,' said Faye.

'Adolescence,' I replied coolly.

'See?' said Faye. 'I *was* listening.' She glanced at her watch. 'Anyway, time's up.' She yawned, stretched and stood up. 'Interesting. *Very* interesting.'

'So what do you think?' I said.

'Whoa there,' said Faye. 'Not so fast. I have to process the information. This could take *years*.' She pinched my cheek playfully and made for the exit. 'Same time next week?'

'Now just hold on a minute,' I said. 'I need something now, Doctor. This is driving me crazy.' And I don't know what it was – most likely the unintentional but legitimising use of the term doctor – but she turned and walked back to the couch.

'I can see that,' she said. She sat down, suppressed a yawn and stroked an imaginary beard. 'Now let me see. Hmn. Interesting. *Very* interesting.'

'I know,' I said. 'We've had that bit.'

'Quiet *please*,' said Faye. 'I'm processing.'

That too, I thought, but what can you do? 'Sorry.'

Faye suddenly sat up. 'Got it,' she said. 'Now why didn't I think of it before?' She made eye contact for the first time. Pretty frightening, to be honest. She's an odd woman. 'The young boy,' she said, 'is you.'

'Me?! But – what about the monk bit?'

'Monk shmunk. Forget the monk bit. Blaise was lying. The point is, the boy was you. Because you and Blaise are soul mates, linked to each other before time and after time. Not to mention the bit in the middle. So the young boy in the dream is you, desperate to make a connection with the woman he won't meet in the real world for many, many years and after much, much searching.'

'You mean – '

'Yes. I do mean. Remember your adolescence. Were you happy?'

'Only when I was – '

'Exactly. QED. I'll invoice you. Better still, give me your bank details, I'll invoice myself.'

Costly it may have been for a two hour session, but I was greatly buoyed by this excellent news. I *was* that boy. Beautiful, soulful eyes? Flop of hair? Yes, indeedy! That was me all right.

'*You're* looking very pleased with yourself,' said Blaise as we lay in bed that night. 'So what did your analyst have to say?'

'The confidentiality of the couch,' I said. 'Remember?' I ruffled her hair affectionately. 'Sweet dreams, and if you happen to meet *a certain person*, be my guest.'

'What *do* you mean?' said Blaise, but before I could elaborate she was sound asleep, a soft smile on her full and honeyed lips.

Faye dropped by the following morning. I found them giggling in the living room. They stopped as soon as I sauntered in. 'Carry on,' I said. 'Don't mind me. Or perhaps I should say' – and I aimed this one squarely at my analyst – 'don't mind *us*.'

A Brisk Hike Up The Trossachs

It is a truth universally acknowledged that marriage is nothing more than legalised prostitution. Which is why I proposed to Blaise. She turned me down, which I took at the time to be feminism gone mad. The truth, however, was far, far worse. It involved her mother, a bath ejector seat, and the idyllic hamlet of Trossach. But let's begin with the mother.

The phone rang. It was Blaise's mother. Blaise promised to be right over. 'So what is it now?' I asked, which brings us to the bath ejector seat. Blaise's mother was, apparently, a big fan of daytime television. I say *apparently* because I'd never actually met her. But according to Blaise, she liked nothing better than to cruise the shopping channels and make a bid for the very latest in gadgetry.

'Her bath ejector seat is stuck,' said Blaise. 'And she's stuck with it. The water is cooling fast, she can't reach the hot tap, so there you have it. I've got to go over.'

'That's the third time this week,' I said. 'I'll go with you.' And before she could protest I raised my hand for silence. 'I won't go anywhere near the woman,' I said. 'But I could do with a breath of fresh air.'

I rooted out my climbing boots and dusted down my signed copy of that timeless classic of travel writing, *A Brisk Hike Up The Trossachs* by Hector Baden Powell, maternal grand-nephew of the world's oldest boy scout[2]. I was soon lost in its exquisite, not to say *limpid*, prose.

'Ready?' said Blaise, who wasn't altogether happy about me making the trip.

I closed my book, saluted in time-honoured Boy Scout fashion, and marched to the car, my imaginary shorts creased to perfection, my hair parted neatly and my two chubby cheeks, also imaginary, puffed up with youthful pride. To say nothing of the kiss curl.

Blaise eased her 1959 Vulva into whatever it is you do with cars, and we were off. It was a race against time. The water, once warm, was probably now tepid and would, also probably, shortly be cold. Blaise gripped the steering wheel, a sure sign of the onset of one of her dreaded migraines. I had looked this up recently in my well-thumbed copy of *Women's Bodies, Men's Wisdom*, and had been referred to 'Abstention From Sexual Intercourse, Excuses For', but decided to keep this nugget of wisdom to myself.

'Haven't you got your medication?' I asked, but I was only fooling myself. I knew what was coming next.

'I think it might be a sugar low,' she said in her small voice. 'Better stop at a garage and get something. Just to be on the safe side.'

'A nice banana, perhaps,' I quipped. My tone was pretty heavy on the irony. 'On the other hand, we just might find something' – I whipped open the glove compartment and a mountain of chocolate tumbled to the floor – 'in here.'

---

[2] His frequent references to the female sex as 'an inexcusable aberration' may, perhaps, jar with the modern reader, but set against this his delightful passages on nature, as witness his exhilarating chapter on rolling naked in gorse with the prettier members of 'F' troop.

'Ah,' said Blaise. 'I've been meaning to mention that.'

'No need,' I replied, my voice hard yet compassionate. 'So what can I get you? Hmn? I can do dark, white, milk. You can have squares, balls, bars. There's – '

'Just give me chocolate,' whimpered Blaise.

I passed her a miniature Milky Way and awaited a progress report with interest.

'That's better,' she sighed. 'Just in time.' She squeezed my hand. 'Thanks, Doctor.' I chuckled softly. No excuses tonight. I held that thought for the remainder of the journey and entered Trossach in excellent spirits.

Blaise left me in the town centre and apologised yet again. 'It really isn't the right time to meet Mother,' she said. 'She's got issues with the Irish.'

'I thought your father was Irish,' I said, adjusting my gaiters with a gay flourish.

'He was. But he kept quiet about it. Here, take my mobile. I'll phone you when I'm through.'

And she was off.

Trossach. You can almost smell the exclamation mark. I was here for the brisk hike, but what a joy simply to breathe the sharp, clear air of this much loved retirement spot; celebrated worldwide for the annual porridge tossing championships, its main claim to immortality rests with the 1950's classic TV series *The Embalmers*.

As I strolled along Main Street I was transported back to those carefree days of childhood and the flickering box in the corner of the room. Every Sunday night Messrs. Mummer and Grieve would traipse the grainy hills and glens touting for business while Janet McNee, dear, prim Janet McNee, tended to their inner man.

'You haven't lived, laddie, till you've sunk your teeth into Janet McNee's Clootie Dumpling, or sniffed the gentle aroma of her Cullen Skink.'

Trossach was black and white in those days. The show didn't survive the advent of colour television – audiences found Mummer's purple nose unintentionally funny – but the series lived on through the loyalty of the fans, and I was watching a coach load of Janet McNees, with their neat grey perms and starched aprons, disgorging onto the town square, waving their spirtles with abandon, when Blaise's mobile rang. The ring tone was set to the high-pitched cackle of a malevolent child.

'Thank goodness I've got you, Dr. O'Shaughnessy,' bellowed Blaise in a voice normally reserved for her mother.

Two points worth mentioning here. I'm not a doctor. My name is not O'Shaughnessy.

'I'm terribly sorry,' I bellowed back. 'I think you've got the wrong number.'

Blaise adjusted her volume. 'Hold on.' I heard her booming at her mother. Something about signals and taking this outside and I do wish you'd use your hearing aid. Moments later she was hissing down the line. 'We've got a problem,' she said. 'Mother's toe is stuck in the bath ejector seat, the water's freezing and I can't get her out on my own.'

'Excellent,' I said. 'At last I get to meet her. I'll bring scones.'

'She's in the bath,' said Blaise in a measured way. 'Anyway, I've told her my doctor is holidaying in the area. So get something for hypothermia, *Doctor*, and please don't dawdle.'

'Doctor?' I said. 'I don't follow.'

'I just don't think it's the right time for her to know about you yet. Trust me.'

'So where's your doctor from?'

'What?'

'Well he can't very well be Irish, now can he?'

'Don't complicate matters,' said Blaise. 'Doctors are supposed to be Irish. So no silly voices. Just hurry.' End of conversation.

I bought a miniature Isle of Ulay single malt and made my way to the house. Past a gateway with Presbyterian iconography. Up the gravel path. Blaise opened the door.

Such beauty. Framed in the jamb she looked like an iconic painting by one of those pre-Raphaelites. We would make love later, of course, but first there was the small matter of her mother.

'Ah, Doctor,' bellowed Blaise. 'Good of you to come.'

'All part of the service,' I said. 'So where's the lucky patient?'

Blaise ushered me into the bathroom. 'Mother,' she bellowed. 'It's Dr. O'Shaughnessy.'

Isobel sat in the bath chittering away like a six-year-old. Not exactly the hewn-granite Calvinist I'd been led to expect. She reminded me of my beloved daughter Bonnie as a child when I left her in the tub and got sidetracked.

'I see you've put in bubble bath,' I said. 'That's a relief.' I removed my jacket and rolled up my sleeves. 'We'll have you free in no time.'

Isobel stopped chattering for a suspicious moment and eyed me keenly. 'Are you Irish?' she said.

'Certainly not,' I replied. 'I'm from Birmingham, but

I got elocution lessons off a Mrs. O'Reilly.' She seemed reassured. 'Right,' I said. 'Let's winch you out of there.'

'I don't think so, Doctor,' said Isobel, scooping a protective layer of bubbles around her upper torso. With, I would have to say, a slightly hunted look.

'Relax,' I said. 'I'm Bush Baptist. I assure you I won't take pleasure in it.'

And with that I plunged my hands deep into the suds and rummaged.

The toe I could fix, it was a simple matter of angles and leverage, but I felt this might be a good opportunity to spend some quality time with its owner, get to know her a little better. I turned to Blaise. 'Is there a monkey wrench in the house?'

Blaise narrowed her eyes. 'I'll have a look in the tool shed,' she said, and left me, arms flailing about in the water.

Her mother gave me a jaundiced look. I felt the need to say something.

'Hypothermia,' I said, 'and, unless I'm very much mistaken, frozen toe.'

'You *are* Irish, aren't you?' said Isobel.

'Sadly, I replied, 'yes.'

'From the North, perhaps?' I detected a faint note of hope.

'I'm afraid not. Tragic accident of birth. Nor,' I sighed, 'am I Bush Baptist.'

Isobel pursed her chattering lips. 'You'll be telling me next you're Romish.'

I decided the time had come for truth, if not reconciliation. 'I can't lie to you, Isobel. I was raised a lapsed Catholic.'

At which point Blaise came back in brandishing a toasting fork. 'Will this do?'

'I don't think we're going to need it after all, Nurse,' I said. 'It's a simple matter of angles. Not to mention, without wishing to get too technical about it, leverage.'

'In that case, Doctor,' said Blaise, 'if you lift, I'll release the toe.'

I leaned towards her mother in what I took to be the accepted bathside manner.

'Trust me,' I soothed. 'I'm fully certified.'

Within moments I'd plopped her down on the mat and she scurried, still chattering, into the living room. I followed her through.

'Nice and warm in here,' I observed. 'At the same time, it might be an idea to put something on.' Which she did. Soon she was steaming gently in front of the fire with a blanket draped round her and a glass of 'medicine' in her aged hand. As she sat there with her skin arranged in neat wrinkles I was reminded of little Bonnie when I finally remembered to take her out of the bath. So – *vulnerable*.

She took another sip of her medicine and gave me the beady eye.

'I'd offer you something, Doctor, but this is a dry house.'

'And I'd put the kettle on,' said Blaise, 'but I'm sure the doctor has other calls on his time.'

'Not at all,' I said. 'Free as a bird. Tea would be lovely.'

Blaise gave me a withering look and went into the kitchen.

Which left me alone with Isobel.

As she glowered at me across the hearth I felt we were

beginning to bond.

'If Mingus wasn't working so hard he'd be here,' she said meaningfully, taking another sip. 'Mingus would be straight over.'

'So – who's this Mingus?' I asked nonchalantly. At least it was meant to be nonchalant, but nonchalance doesn't contain within its broader meaning a mounting sense of doom.

Isobel took another dainty sip. 'Why, Blaise's husband,' she said, pointing to a wall of photos. Blaise in a wedding dress. Blaise cutting a wedding cake. Blaise being driven away in a wedding car. All with the same – husband?

I was speechless. I thought of all those times she'd been away overnight. Readings, she'd said. Seminars. Book signings. And all the time – surely it couldn't be possible – she'd been leading a double life.

Isobel broke the silence. 'He's a chief executive.' I was still speechless, so I said nothing. 'Oh, yes indeed,' she continued, sipping her medicine with Lutheran abandon. 'He's very high up is Mingus.'

I could finally contain myself no longer.

'Blaise is – married?'

'Happily, Doctor. Ecstatically.'

Blaise came back in, beautiful still but now, perhaps, unattainable. I was devastated. I accepted the cup of tea she proffered – as an unacceptable substitute for true love – and mentally packed my bags.

Isobel took another sip and giggled quietly.

'For goodness sake, Mother,' said Blaise. 'What have you been saying to upset the doctor? Just look at his little face.'

Ah. If only she knew.

Her mother took a generous slurp.

'He wouldn't have had to come in the first place,' she pouted, 'if my favourite son-in-law was here.'

Blaise bristled. 'Who?!'

'You know very well who,' I said frostily, pointing at the wall of photos. 'Mingus.'

'Mother,' snapped Blaise gently. 'I haven't seen Mingus in 12 years.'

Her mother shifted uneasily.

'That'll be the overtime.'

'No,' said Blaise. 'That'll be the divorce.' She stood up. 'And besides, I should have told you before, Mother. I've got a new man in my life.'

Her mother swirled the medicine in her glass and mulled this over. She lowered her voice to a melancholy whisper. 'There's something I've been wanting to tell you too, Blaise. The good doctor has brought it all back and, well, now's as good a time as any. Maybe you'd best sit down.'

Blaise stayed rooted to the spot. 'What is it, Mother?'

'It's been weighing on me for years. Your father' – Isobel, her eyes misty, suddenly looked her age – 'was Irish. There, I've said it.'

The weight lifted, she sat up straight in her seat. 'So where's this fancy man of yours just now?'

'At home,' said Blaise. 'Why?'

Her mother staggered to her feet. 'I'm an old woman,' she hiccupped, 'A bit set in my ways. But maybe it's time.'

She gave her medicine a final swirl, drained the glass, and picked up the phone.

'Mother?' said Blaise.

'Let me be, lass,' insisted her mother. 'Now where's that blessed number of yours?'

She dialled. The malevolent child cackled in my pocket. I steeled myself, stood, and looked at the woman I loved.

'Leave this to me, Blaise,' I said. '*I'll* take it.'

Soggy Bottom Baby

The queue in the chemist's wasn't happy. The assistant wasn't happy. I was about to get furious. At this stage, however, I was in complete control.

'The word escapes me at present,' I said, 'but it's related to women and it's got 'men' in it.'

'Menstruation?' suggested the assistant.

'Not menstruation.'

'Hymen?'

'Nope.'

'Women?'

'Not women.'

'How about mental?' muttered the man behind me. 'That's got men in it.'

'Not' – and I was getting a bit testy at this stage – 'mental.'

Just then the manageress came over. 'What seems to be the trouble?' she enquired.

Several people gave their versions, I gave mine.

'Menopause,' she said.

'That's the one. Now here's the problem in embryo. I bought these condom 12-packs, buy two get one free. So far, so excellent. I'd just begun to open the wrapper on *this*, the free packet, prior to – well, let's not go into that. There are ladies present. Anyway, no sooner had I begun than the one true love of my life said 'Whoa, not so fast, big boy. We won't be needing *those* again.' The manageress looked confused. 'Menopause, see?' I explained. 'So I thought, great. Refund or, at the very least, credit slip.'

'But this packet's partially open,' said the manageress, picking it up and peering at it.

'Ah yes,' I replied, 'but that, as I've just explained to this charming young sales assistant, 'is the *free* one.'

'I'm sorry,' she said, handing me the packet back, 'but it doesn't work like that.'

'In that case,' I replied, stuffing it back into my coat, 'I'll just have to find a young woman of childbearing age and, not to put too fine a point on it, use 'em up.'

I was being heavily ironical. I hate waste, but not to the extent of splitting up with the one true et cetera.

Naturally, I filled Blaise in when I got home.

'And there you have it,' I concluded. 'Three packets of condoms. No use to us.'

'Never mind about that now,' said Blaise, punching the cushions and generally manhandling the furniture. 'Bonnie phoned earlier. She's on her way.'

Bonnie! My beloved daughter. Coming to see her beloved dad. This was wonderful news. I reflected that I hadn't seen my little girl for some time – her choice, not mine – so her decision to visit was totally unexpected.

'Tell you what,' I enthused, 'this is a wonderful opportunity to finish her book. It's the last thing she'll be expecting.'

Now, as Blaise is a successful author I'm normally wary of mentioning my own writing efforts. But when Bonnie was a toddler I'd started work on an illustrated story about her and, such was my meticulous attention to detail, I'd never got round to finishing it.

'Are you sure that's a good idea?' said Blaise, violently

plumping a bean bag.

I waved all doubts aside. 'She'll thank me for it. Trust me. You think I don't know my own daughter?'

'Hmn,' said Blaise, and she said it again when I showed her my work in progress.

See Soggy Bottom Baby!
See her spanking brand new potty!!!

'It started as a toilet training manual,' I explained.

'Hmn,' said Blaise, flicking through the pages.

'Sorry, what are you implying?' I asked.

'She's nearly seventeen,' she said. 'Are you seriously thinking of giving this to your seventeen year old daughter?'

'Well, I've got to finish it first, and I think I've worked out how to do it. I've got to get her sitting on that blessèd potty.'

Blaise put her arms around me and held me close.

'Don't do this,' she sighed.

Professional jealousy? Two Writers In Same House Syndrome? Difficult to tell. I kissed her menopausal forehead and disengaged. There was work to be done – and what work!

I'm always a little bit in awe of professional writers. All those words, and all of them so carefully – *arranged*. I had the added difficulty of the illustrations, although I freely admit I have absolutely no talent in that department, and it certainly showed. But the words. *There* was the challenge. It's all very well to say 'Get her on that blessèd potty', but you've got to make it aesthetically pleasing. Connect the botty to the potty in 8 pages of seamless prose, one sentence max per page.

Easier said than done.

I'd read all the books on the subject. Character arcs. Motivation. Structure. I even had a sub-plot of the disintegrating marriage working away in the background. But unless you know what's going on in that toddler's head – forget it.

I realised early on that the sub-plot, or, should I say *main* sub-plot, was Chekhovian in its themes of love, loss, the passing of the old order and, for some reason, the desire to move to Moscow. That was the easy bit. But I had to think myself into the mind of the child. Did the potty, for instance, have symbolic meaning beyond its essential self? Was there a possible Holy Grail motif at work here? Or were we talking rites of passage? To be honest, the story had begun to assume the timeless relevance of ancient myth and I was wondering – aloud, apparently – if the film version would respect the integrity of the text when the doorbell rang.

I downed tools – my biro in this case – and leapt into action.

I had assumed that my ex-wife would be dropping little Bonnie off. Last time I'd seen Dolores two decades of wedded bliss and a nervous breakdown had taken their toll.

I opened the door. 'Dolores,' I gushed. 'You look positively youthful.'

'Hi, Dad. Love the grey rinse.' With that Bonnie brushed past me into the flat.

Blaise didn't seem as surprised as I was at the growth spurt. Apparently young people are like that these days, and my immediate thought was 'I hope they get on together, Bonnie and Blaise'. I know what women are like, and I didn't want them fighting like tomcats. But I needn't have worried.

'Wow,' said Bonnie as soon as she saw Blaise. 'It really IS you. The FAMOUS AUTHOR! My friends will be sooooooooo GUTTED!'

Before I had time to correct her on the grey rinse front, Bonnie had entered Blaise's study – out of bounds to *me*, I hasten to add – and was shrieking and giggling and referring to pretty well everything in there as AWESOME.

I heard all this from the safety of the bathroom. Bonnie had seen fit to close the study door on my face and I was getting used to the fact that her bonding with Blaise had gone better than I'd hoped. I was about to tear myself away from the bathroom mirror with the sad realisation that my hair was indeed verging on *Hint of Grey*, when Blaise's mobile rang. The shrieks and giggling stopped.

Silence for a moment.

Grey, I mused. Gravitas. Same Latin root? I never did find out.

Next thing, I heard Blaise's door open.

'Just stay where you are,' she bellowed into her mobile. 'I'll be right over.'

I came out of the bathroom.

'Your mother,' I said. I wasn't asking. I knew it was her mother. 'Don't tell me. She's been watching daytime television. She's seen yet another gadget. She's bought it and, yet again, she's got herself stuck.'

'It's her new indoor ski lift,' sighed Blaise. 'It's stuck halfway up the stairs and she can't climb down.'

'I'll get my coat,' I said.

'Best if you stay here,' said Blaise. She turned to Bonnie. 'My mother has issues with your father.'

'Join the queue,' muttered Bonnie.

They both giggled. Queue? I thought. What queue? But I said nothing, and soon I was consoling myself with the fond thought that this would give me an excellent opportunity to finish *Soggy Bottom Baby*. Perhaps even colour in the pictures.

I waved them off, went back into the flat, and was just passing Blaise's study when I noticed that the Internet had been left on. Another drowned polar bear, I chuckled, and ventured in to switch it off. But just as I reached for the mouse my eye was caught by the screen.

myincrediblycomplicatedlifedotsomethingdotsomething

I knew the feeling.

I was soon drawn in, seduced by the artless prose, the appalling punctuation, the unorthodox orthography. What is it with kidz these daze? Having said that, I must admit I found the energy refreshing and unintentionally comic.

I was just thinking that, in spite of the writer's best efforts, the character known as Dysfunctional Dad was coming across as the epitome of cool, when one of those chat line messages popped up. 'U still there?' it read.

Hmph. I wasn't too impressed with that. 'Me still here,' I typed wittily. Or so I thought.

'Me still here 2. Like, wot's happnin?'

Right. That was it. The wit of my riposte had been lost on the recipient, and it awakened the traditionalist in me, that long dormant hungering for spit, polish and blue blazers that lurks beneath my louche exterior. 'Now look here,' I replied, and I was off. I began my dissertation with a brief defence of one endangered species, the transitive verb, which segued neatly into a witty funeral oration for another, the subordinate clause. I then broadened my elegiac rant from the particular to the general – grammar; rules of – before getting to the nub of the problem, in which I bemoaned, with much flailing of arms and spittle in the grand rhetorical tradition of Cicero and his ilk, the absence of Latin on the school syllabus.

I double-checked my message for typographical errors, pruned the central section of some of its more fanciful asides, and clicked *send*. I foolishly expected a considered response. 'U on somefink?' was not that response.

But enough of my Utopian visionary side. Tempus was fugiting fast. I still had to finish Bonnie's story and my idea for the final frame, some time later, was simplicity itself. Soggy Bottom Baby plonks her botty on the potty. Perfect. Well, almost. She's still wearing her nappy. This allowed for a follow-up and, depending on the success of the franchise, a possible series. I chortled wildly to myself at the sheer giddy joy of being a tax exile, and had just settled down with a set of crayons for the all-important visuals when the ladies returned.

Bonnie headed straight for Blaise's study. Seconds later, she let rip with a wail of blood-chilling intensity, of almost heartbreaking anguish. Catastrophe! I thought. She's impaled herself on the swivel chair!

I raced to the rescue, but the cause of her outburst, it

turned out, was slightly less fatal. Bonnie's online pals, it seems, had merely questioned her sanity. Blaise, who had followed at a more leisurely pace, gave me one of those odd looks that she reserves for, well, *me*. She then clapped her hands with possibly forced jollity.

'Tell you what,' she said brightly, 'why don't you two spend some quality time together. Go for a coffee. I'll sign some books for Bonnie's friends.' Bonnie, however, seemed reluctant. 'Come on, Bonnie,' said Blaise. 'What can possibly happen between here and the coffee shop?'

'You don't know Dad,' sulked Bonnie.

Blaise sighed. 'Oh, but I do. I *do*.'

No help there, because Bonnie was off. 'We were at the beach, right? And he was wearing these – ' Words failed her.

'Bathing trunks?' I suggested helpfully.

'I mean *everything* was showing,' wailed Bonnie.

'Surely not *everything*,' said Blaise.

'Okay.' said Bonnie. 'Maybe not *everything*. But everything *else*.'

Blaise, my love and my defender against all attempts at character assassination, sighed deeply. 'Well, never mind about that now,' she said. 'Look, he has his trousers on.'

She thrust Bonnie's coat at her and bundled us out of the flat.

Bonding would come at the coffee shop, but first Bonnie wanted to pop into the chemist for, as she put it, 'women's things'. I waited at the counter and gazed upon her in wonder as she riffled the shelves. 'Women's things.' My little girl.

But not so little any more. She had metamorphosed,

transmogrified, grown – that's the word! – into a beautiful young woman. And I? Well, time perhaps to think of a subtle tint.

I was toying with the idea of the self-applied blond streak when I spotted the manageress eyeing me from the safety of the cash register. Time to build bridges, I felt. I puffed up with pride as a heavily laden Bonnie bore down on the till.

'Aren't they just beautiful at that age,' I beamed, producing my credit card. 'So young. So lovely.'

Bonnie plopped her basket down on the counter. The manageress, however, had eyes for me alone.

'You ought to be *ashamed* of yourself,' she hissed. 'People like you' – and she paused for maximum effect – 'disgust me.'

As I left the shop and went in search of Bonnie – so like her mother – I reflected that I probably wouldn't see her again for several years. But as Blaise, my love and my soul mate, pointed out over steaming mugs of cocoa as we sat in bed that night, it would give me plenty of time to colour in her book.

Death of a Ladle's Man

Due to a typing error I was once referred to as 'a great man for the ladles'. All that changed as soon as I met Blaise. But have I ever strayed from the path of fidelity? Hard to tell.

Take, for example, the following: Blaise and I were about to fly to Dublin. Sin city. We would no doubt meet thousands of people en route, many of them female, so before we set off I resolved to be faithful to the love of my life in thought, word and deed. But my libido had a mind of its own.

All went well at first. The check-in staff was young and female but, luckily for me, their hair was scraped back from their foreheads and tied into buns, which took me right back to the primary school teachers of my childhood. Not the women of my more dubious dreams, frankly, and my libido agreed. In a funny sort of way we bonded over this, so in the boredom of the interminable queue I decided to give my libido a name.

'How about Randy?' it said.

'Great idea,' I replied. *'Fintan.'*

We name things to control them. Fintan. Prim. Top button always fastened. That should keep it quiet.

Which it did. Until, that is, a statuesque American woman approached Blaise at the coffee stand. 'I am just *such* an admirer of your poetic oeuvre,' she gushed.

'Why, *thank* you,' gushed Blaise.

Fintan undid his top button. 'Kinda hot in here,' he smirked.

Pretty soon the woman was gushing at Blaise and Blaise was gushing at the woman. Which presented me with a problem. The woman was, to all conventional ways of thinking, stunningly attractive. Curves. Curves within curves. Not my type – Blaise is my type – but Fintan had worked out for himself that she was a good five eleven, which meant that, scarlet high heels included, her generous cleavage stood at eye level. My eye level.

I excused myself and decided to take Fintan off to browse at the airport bookshop. I was about to search for *Self Help* when I noticed a man in a wheelchair gazing plaintively at the magazine rack. Believe me, I know plaintive when I see it, even if it *was* the back view.

At a glance I could see what his problem was. Lack of leverage. Obviously unable to reach the pornography which, let's say, graced the top shelf. I'm not a pornography lover myself. Au contraire. But neither am I heightist. I decided, on the spot, to patent the telescopic wheelchair. In the short term, however, I grabbed a bundle of magazines at random and thrust them at my wheelchair-bound friend.

'Not to my taste,' I said, 'but enjoy.'

Fintan was now two buttons down. I tugged him away from the front cover of *Solo – The Magazine For The Hard Of Bonking*, and eased him towards 'Theology'.

It was limited to a lone copy of *The Plain Truth*, and I was busy reading the editorial when I overheard the man in the wheelchair deep in conversation with his wife.

'If you can reach up for smut, Declan,' she spat, 'you can push your own feckin' wheelchair.'

'But – ,' he complained, 'but that is so un*fair*.'

'Don't tell me,' sneered his wife. 'A big boy gave you

the magazines and ran away.'

'He wasn't that big,' whined the man. He lowered his voice for maximum sympathy. 'He just wasn't in a wheelchair.'

'I see,' said his wife. 'So what did this sleazeball look like, because I'll tell you one thing, he'll be in a feckin' wheelchair when *I've* finished with him.'

'I didn't actually *see* him,' whimpered Declan. 'But I'd recognize the voice anywhere. North Dublin. Clontarf.'

'Street and house number available on request, I suppose,' sneered his wife.

'As it happens, yes,' he said, and I have to say he was uncannily accurate. He was also uncannily accurate as to the year the voice left Ireland and where it had been since.

'Sure what would I want with smut anyway?' he whimpered. 'Sure amn't I blind?'

Declan's wife gave him a filthy look which may well have been lost on the poor man. 'So you say.'

I always think that it's not the one incident that wrecks a marriage. No. It's a constant build up of small grudges. I reflected that the magazine spat was merely the icing on the divorce cake, and besides, the disintegration of a once-loving relationship is an intensely private thing. So I left them to it and returned to Blaise. The American fan, I noted with relief, was being statuesque with her cleavage elsewhere.

'I was beginning to wonder where you'd got to,' said Blaise. 'But what a lovely young woman. Wasn't she just stunning!'

'*Whoo,*' said Fintan, undoing the third button down.

I said nothing.

'Wouldn't surprise me, all the same,' said Blaise,

lowering her voice, 'if she's had her breasts enhanced.'

And before Fintan had a chance to lower the tone, I was in there.

'Breasts?' I said. 'What breasts?'

Some time later we'd taken our seats on the plane. Blaise's fan was in the row in front, but at least, I mused, that meant her breasts were pointing the right way.

'The wrong way,' sulked Fintan, reconsidering his third button.

I'd just established the presence of the in-flight magazine – a pleasure deferred – and was weighing up the merits and demerits of sucking a mint before we took off, when a hen party came on board, shrieking and cackling, and dived on the nearby seats. One of them hoicked her bag into the overhead locker to reveal a luminous, lime-green, see-through thong.

I recoiled, Fintan ogled. Another button. He was beginning to look like a Latin crooner on his day off.

'Relax,' he slavered, ruffling his own chest hair. *'I'm only trying to read the label.'*

I averted both our gazes while Blaise, oblivious, thank goodness, indulged in a surreptitious chocolate. The woman extinguished her thong, I opened *The Plain Truth* at the problem page, Fintan yawned, and we settled in for an uneventful flight. I clicked my safety belt shut.

And then? Ye Gods! My worst nightmare. Moving in my direction along the aisle came an old flame from my wild, bohemian mid-forties. As I glanced over at Blaise trying to unwrap an illicit truffle, I was filled with foreboding. I'd never tested Blaise on the jealous rage front, but an old girlfriend under the same aluminium roof? We were treading delicate ground here. Blaise looked reasonably placid at that point, but she's a martyr to the menopausal mood. This could well lead to her terrifying speciality, the Celtic Hot Flush.

As my ex-girlfriend inched closer, the memories, unbidden, flooded back. Birmingham. City of Endless Love. It was definitely her. Same regal bearing. Same burka. I'd recognize those glasses anywhere. Fortunately Blaise was still busy unwrapping, so my cold sweat went unnoticed. For now. Fatima, struggling with a hefty piece of hand luggage, stopped at our row. Blaise nudged me. 'You might want to help that woman with her bag.'

'That woman' was standing a matter of centimetres away. Closer than we'd ever got in our relationship. I was too stunned to move. I risked being discovered and possibly losing my life in the process. A tad overdramatic? Perhaps. But here's the nightmare scenario. Fatima recognises me and, simultaneously, Blaise's chocolates run out.

A grunt reminiscent of the Wimbledon ladies' singles' final told me Fatima's bag was up, but Blaise wouldn't let the matter rest.

'What's wrong with you?' she whispered. 'You're usually so helpful. Even when it's not required.'

She could have been referring to any number of incidents, but I didn't draw her out. A flap of black material from my ex-girlfriend's burka had just brushed against my knee. And my ex-girlfriend was in it.

What could I do? I had no idea how Blaise would react if she knew I was sitting beside a woman I'd once passionately wooed in Birmingham, City of Endless Love. Accompanied at all times, as Fintan dryly pointed out, by her five brothers.

Fatima squeezed in beside me. There was only one thing for it. I closed my eyes and pretended to nod off. It worked. As the plane rose above the clouds I drifted slowly into sleep. I dreamed that Fintan, my libidinous libido, was disappearing down a giant cleavage and screaming at me to throw him something. I tossed him a rope, but no. He wanted a back copy of *Solo*. As it was a dream I just happened to have the latest issue, hot off the press. I was about to pass it over when a primary school teacher with a giant bun grabbed hold of the magazine and turned on me.

'So that's the way it is, Mister,' she admonished, bearing slowly down on me, undoing her bun with predatory intent. The sun set behind her huge pinched face as she loomed over me in a terrifying parody of German expressionist cinema.

'Come to Aine,' she snarled.

As she shook the bun-hair free her face relaxed, its liberated jowls flopping earthward. Fintan bounced happily on the giant cleavage. A huge black moon bathed Aine in an eerie half-light. She reached down to grab hold of me with long-suppressed lust and –

I awoke with a jolt. An air hostess was leaning over my seat, her bun still tight in place. 'Would you like something from the bar?' she said. I sank further into my seat. I wasn't ready for that much reality.

Fintan, however, was. *'Will you look at the size of those – Phwoar!'* he drooled, fondling several buttons at once.

'Breasts?' I blurted. 'What breasts?'

'You're awake,' mumbled Blaise, scooping chocolate wrappers guiltily off her lap.

Fatima hadn't moved in all this time. I sneaked a sideways glance. She was reading the in-flight magazine. *'Ireland's Most Eligible Bachelors.'* She seemed engrossed, and suddenly I was overcome with a great sadness. Trip to Ireland? This article? She was obviously going to Dublin in search of a replacement me.

As we flew over Belfast and turned left my mind wound back to the arranged separation all those years ago. Courtesy of her brothers. I brooded on this till the plane started its descent. Touched down in Dublin. Cruised to a halt.

The overhead lockers opened. Fatima yanked her luggage out and headed down the aisle with nary a backward glance. I was so relieved I almost undid *my* top button. Blaise nudged me out of my seat. I tried to move but Fintan was transfixed by the curvaceous American fan. 'After *you*,' he smarmed, undoing most of his remaining buttons.

'Stop *ogling*,' hissed Blaise.

No point in explaining the situation, so I moved on. The queue filed slowly out, along the aisle, past the hostesses who were charm itself. *Bye now. Thanks indeed. Safe onward journey.* They were so young. So sweet looking. Such – tidy hair. There was nothing else for it. I *had* to make amends for my appalling dream.

'Nice buns, ladies,' I said, flashing them an avuncular smile. The older hostess scowled, the younger one reached for her phone. The statuesque American turned at the exit. 'Buns, huh? The way he's been ogling me the whole goddam flight, I kinda had him figured for a breast man.'

I cringed and tried to explain myself, but Blaise dragged me out of the plane.

'What's got into you?' she hissed as we crossed the tarmac, a few paces behind Fatima. 'You've been acting like some kind of pervert.'

Fintan smirked shamelessly. I was mumbling incoherently in a desperate attempt to explain the inexplicable when a cop car raced towards us, siren blaring. I steeled myself for my imminent arrest. The inevitable hand on the shoulder. The reading of rights. The humiliating hand-cuffs. But things were about to take an interesting twist. As the car squealed to a halt, Fatima lashed out with her luggage and made a break for it. Hampered by her burka, however, she was brought down within yards by a couple of burly Gardaí. In the struggle her headscarf came off. Fatima – and I had to rethink my attitude to Birmingham here – was a man.

That night, as I lay in bed with Blaise, I had to come to terms with my troubled past. Eighteen months in Birmingham, City of Endless Love, with an undercover transvestite. No wonder her brothers stepped in.

Things were so much simpler now, I reflected, as I prepared for a night of endless love in Dublin, Ireland's answer to Birmingham.

Or were they?

Fintan, bane of my life, appeared at the end of the bed, preening shamelessly, and ripped his pyjama top off.

Buttons everywhere.

'Threesome!' he roared, dive-bombing the bed.

I thwacked him with malice aforethought high over the bedpost, moved towards my one true love, and gently kissed the remains of a nut cluster from her upper lip.

Some things are not meant for sharing.

The Thing You Did Last Time

I rapped on Blaise's study door with a loud rat-a-tat-tat.

'Blaise,' I called. 'The door seems to be jammed.' Silence. 'Could you try it from your side.' Silence. 'Please.'

The door opened and a chastened Blaise peered out. 'It was locked,' she said, pointing at a large sign. *Please Do Not Disturb.*

'Ah,' I said. 'Hadn't thought of that.' To be honest I hadn't noticed. Another of her efforts to keep her monstrous regiment of so-called friends at bay, no doubt. She further pointed to a rather witty footnote[3]. I laughed appreciatively.

'So is it working?' I asked.

'Not really,' she replied. 'No.'

'Well I'm not totally surprised,' I said. 'If pretty blatant signs have no effect I can't see what a footnote is going to do.'

'Or,' she sighed plaintively, 'two Yales and a mortice.'

'Precisely. Anyway, the thing is – '

I stopped in mid-flow. I'd obviously knocked on the door for a reason. But what? Blaise gave me a look. What I call her suffer in silence look. Typical. If I'd been granted immediate access the problem wouldn't have arisen in the first place. I was about to point this out when I noted that she looked tired. Possibly drawn. I decided to change tack.

'You spend far too much time in that room,' I said.

[3] THAT MEANS YOU.

'All those rhyming couplets. It's unnatural.'

Blaise pushed me gently into the hallway. She closed the door softly in my face. We would, I felt, agree to disagree.

Cut to several hours later. At breakfast she'd mentioned some sort of a 'do', on that evening apparently, and I hadn't seen her all afternoon. She was obviously wrestling with the word, so I approached the door again. Still locked. Sign still up. Footnote reinforced by three exclamation marks. I rapped – no answer – and rapped again. Vigorously this time. Knuckle-bruisingly. Nothing.

'Blaise,' I tried. 'Blaise!'

Had she gone to a level of concentration uncharted by mere mortals? Or fallen sound asleep? This was serious. The 'do' she'd mentioned at breakfast had sounded pretty important. Something or other involving the university. She certainly wouldn't want to miss it. Only one thing to do. Phone her. She usually clutched her mobile like a comfort blanket, so I expected a quick breakthrough on the contact front. But life has a way of throwing the odd curve ball, that infuriating little twist that makes us suspect the existence of a higher power with a malicious sense of humour. I grabbed the land line and dialled. Her mobile lit up on the table in front of me and I was on the point of answering the damned thing myself when Blaise rushed out of the bathroom with a sort of frantic glide; a grace born of beauty, with the merest hint of panic.

'Ah, *there* you are,' I said, and I was about to remind her of the pending engagement when she shushed me.

'I'll just get this,' she said, grabbing the mobile. 'Could be about tonight. Hello?'

'Hello,' I replied. 'I thought you were in your study so I phoned.'

She gave her mobile a long-suffering look, seemed to hover on the brink of indecision, then put it back to her ear.

'What is it now?' she said. 'Only I've got to go in about twenty minutes and I still haven't got my face on.'

I let that one pass. This was no time for levity. Besides, I'd noted the *'I've'* not *'We've'*. I arched a quizzical eyebrow in her direction.

'Okay,' she said. 'I've been invited to a soirée at the university. It's being hosted by Professor Letchworth, who just happens to be making the decision on my fellowship.' I may have looked bemused. 'Professor Letchworth? You know? The one with the reputation?' Obviously something to do with the rarefied world of academia because *I'd* never heard of him. 'Anyway,' she said. 'What did you want?'

'Eh?'

'*You* called *me*.'

'Ah. It's about tonight,' I said. 'We've got to go in about twenty minutes.' Blaise gave me the look. She'd noted the *'We've'* not *'I've'*. I raised a hand for kindly-let-me-finish. 'Moral support,' I said. 'You know you need it.'

Blaise sighed the sigh. 'Okay,' she said, gliding back towards the bathroom, 'You're welcome to come – on one condition. Don't do what you did last time!'

As we bopped towards Professor Letchworth's residence in Blaise's 1959 Vulva, her words reverberated in my head.

'You're welcome to come on one condition. *Don't do what you did last time!*'

The first bit I could take. No problem whatsoever with the first bit. The follow up, however, had me stumped on two fronts. What had I done? And what last time? I was brooding on both questions as Blaise pulled up outside her old Alma Mater. In normal circumstances, I would have been transported to another age by the cloisters, the turrets, the undulating lawns, but all they did now was add to my confusion. I'd never been here in my life. Perhaps the thing I did last time was done somewhere else. Her beloved mother's, for instance. Or, and this was a distinct possibility, the thing that was done last time was done here, but not by me. The incident, for all I knew, could have involved her first husband, whose name escapes me at present.

I was wondering whether it was advisable to bring the subject up when Blaise grabbed hold of the magnificent brass doorknob. The sound of her knock echoed through the building with a deep, sonorous boom. I expected an ancient butler with hearing problems and a stoop to arrive some days later, but the door was opened in seconds by a louche type in a linen suit, with a flop of dark curls and a trim goatee beard.

'My dear Blaise,' said Professor Letchworth, staring at the love of my life in an odd sort of way. 'I spotted you from the window. Do come in.' He held his arm out to guide her up the three inch step. 'I see you've brought your chaperone,' he jibed. I held my peace, contenting myself with aiming a couple of pointedly furrowed eyebrows at his departing back.

He continued to guide Blaise – manually – through a dark, wood-panelled hall into an enormous drawing room. I was immediately struck by the plush cream carpet, liberally dotted with chattering academics. Professor Letchworth strode across to the drinks table and, with a flourish and a conspiratorial smile, poured Blaise a glass of wine. Blaise gave me a what-can-you-do look. What indeed? She then described a discreet circle with her index finger. I took this to mean 'Mingle'. I poured myself a glass of sparkling water and prepared to do just that.

As a keen student of humanity there's nothing I like more than a roomful of humans, but I'm more the detached observer type. I'm not a mingler by nature. Besides, to be quite honest I was out of my depth with this lot. I stood on the outskirts of several animated conversations with nothing to add to the intellectual gymnastics on offer. *Way* above my head. Besides, there's only so much linguistic theory one man can take. I began to be – what's the word? – bored. A young woman wandered about with a tray of canapés. I chose a couple of the less miniscule ones and was contemplating a third when I thought 'Ah. Perhaps this is the thing I did last time.' Mindful as I was of my promise to Blaise, I was determined not to do whatever it was. If, indeed, it was me who'd done it.

Which placed certain restrictions on my natural ebullience. I studied the bubbles in my drink for some time. After a while the pattern started to repeat itself. The effect was intensely soporific, and I'd just decided to look further afield for stimulation when Blaise floated towards me across the vast expanse of carpet, followed closely by the good professor.

'Professor Letchworth wants to discuss – ,' said Blaise,

' – a certain little matter,' coughed the professor discreetly. 'In my chambers, if you follow.'

Of course I followed. I almost quipped that Blaise – all going well – would leave a woman and come back a fellow, but didn't want to come across as pre-emptive.

'Want me to come too?' I offered. The moral support card. You never knew.

'That *won't* be necessary,' smiled the professor. 'Really.'

I bade Blaise a fond farewell, and watched them as they left. Curious. The young woman with the canapés seemed to be watching them as well and she looked, I would have to say, pretty upset. The tray tilted dangerously as if to give outward expression to her inner turmoil. I was transported back in time by this poignant little scene to a kinder, gentler century. A member of the servant class with a case of unrequited love for the master. It was that sort of room.

In an effort to take her mind off her obvious distress, I relieved the young woman of several canapés and looked vaguely sympathetic. It may not have mended her broken heart, but at least it took some weight off the tray. I commented favourably on the taste and texture. Small talk, and it usually works. But not this time. She sighed and curtsied. Or perhaps she was just sinking under the weight of her heartbreak, not to mention the rigours of life below stairs. On the positive side, her tray was several centimetres higher. As with a tray so with the human heart. Sometimes the only way is up.

Buoyed by this happy thought I took up position by the magnificent fireplace and returned to the role of bemused observer. The conversations were still, as far as I could understand them, unintelligible. Ah well. Such is the world of the academic. I would have to get used to it. Blaise would soon be joining their ranks. I made a mental note to enjoy the time we had left before she became incomprehensible.

Bored, I was about to seek out a few more canapés when my eye was caught by a dapper little man with a high waistband and prominent name tag – EMERITUS PROFESSOR BRIDIE – shamelessly ogling the magnificent bosom of a large woman in a dazzling floral robe. Odd that I hadn't noticed her before in a roomful of muted tweed – but then I only have eyes for Blaise, as I proposed to tell her when she had the fellowship business sorted out.

The large woman, once noticed, was hard to un-notice. In profile she reminded me of legendary blues shouter Big Mama Thornton, whose *Black Snake Moan* had so traumatised me in my early childhood when it was played in error on Children's Favourites[4]. But back to her bosom. She seemed totally oblivious to its mesmerising effect as she spoke of giving a voice to her people.

'Mind if I squeeze past,' I said. The effect on the large woman was alarming.

'Oh my good gracious *Lord*,' she gushed as I brushed past her heaving amplitude. 'Are you from IRELAND?!"

---

[4] For those interested in such matters, it replaced *I'm a Pink Toothbrush, You're a Blue Toothbrush* by Max, later Sir Max, Bygraves.

'Yes,' I said. 'I am.' No point denying it – how else to explain the soft Irish burr?

Emeritus Professor Bridie hitched his trousers up and gave me a filthy look, while she sighed with uninhibited joy. 'Albertine Bunratty, University of Montserrat,' she said, grabbing a passing bottle. 'But you can call me Tina. Here, let me *fill you up*.'

I held a hand over my glass. 'Not for me, thanks. I'll stick to the old H2O.'

Albertine hooted in disbelief. 'What?! An Irishman who does not *drink*?'

Emeritus Professor Bridie glowered at me and ogled Albertine simultaneously. But Albertine had eyes only for me as she removed my hand and filled my trembling glass. The aroma that assailed my nostrils had a pleasant, slightly pungent bouquet. Linseed. Hint of huckleberry. Leather elbow patches. Although, on mature reflection, that may have been the smell of Bridie's jacket.

I raised the glass to my lips. I was about to take a tentative sip. But wait. Was this the thing I'd done last time? Was the seductive lure of the fermented grape involved? I honestly couldn't remember, which meant that it possibly was. Alcohol can do that to a man[5]. I lowered the glass and made my excuses.

'Well if you won't have a drink,' said Albertine, 'at least sing *Danny Boy*.' I demurred politely, but firmly. I'd left Ireland to get away from the damned thing, but I wasn't telling *her* that.

---

[5] I once sauntered out for a pint of milk in north London and found myself, three weeks later, face down in a gutter with several members of celebrated punk-folk group *The Red-headed Whores From Ringsend*. In my defence, as I pointed out to Blaise in one of our regular truth sessions several decades later, the group in question was all-male. Added to which I prefer chamber music. But still.

'I'm afraid I don't know the words,' I lied.

'What sort of Irishman are you at all?' Albertine pouted playfully, and before I could formulate an answer she grabbed hold of my hand and started to sing the accursed song, in what I have to say was a very pleasing baritone. *I* was now the mesmerised one, sucked into a race memory of sentimentality for which there was no known cure. She closed her eyes and rocked my hand back and forth in rhythm to the plaintive melody. I knew there was no escape and hoped that Blaise wouldn't choose this moment to come back.

But wait! As she approached the first high A, Albertine's emotion overcame her. She clasped both hands to her breast, eyes still firmly shut, and I took advantage of this temporary disengagement to feint to one side. Emeritus Professor Bridie glowered a look of gratitude and grabbed her hand as it descended. I headed out the door as Albertine launched into verse three. The one about *come ye back when summer's in the meadow*. I decided to think about it. But first, a quick breather.

I closed the door as Albertine described the meadow. White with snow, apparently. The hallway, on the other hand, was dark and wood-panelled. Dotted with ancient portraits, it harked back to a bygone age in a curiously reassuring way. The winged collars. The stern, unyielding gazes. All very nineteenth century. The sound of sobbing blended in beautifully with the general ambience, almost as if it had been conjured up from the all-pervading fustiness and gloom. Which it hadn't. It was very much of the present day, and it came from a room at the end of a short corridor.

Not wishing to intrude on private grief I was about

to retrace my steps, but the sobbing grew louder. It was recognisably female. No doubt about it, there *is* a difference. I approached the door gingerly, eased it open. There, in a huge kitchen, surrounded by canapés and now weeping openly, sat the lowly servant girl.

I tiptoed solicitously in. She continued to weep. I went over and put my hand on her shoulder. Empathetically. I could feel her inner turmoil. There was a convenient box of tissues on the table. I passed her one.

'I understand,' I said. 'You're a lowly servant girl, he's the master of the house. A love that can never be.'

She scrunched her face up with bitterness and hurt.

'Lowly servant girl?' she spluttered. 'I'm his *wife*, and he's a philandering bastard.' Now there, I thought, was a twist. I passed her another tissue. She blew her reddening nose. 'I didn't mind when he was philandering with *me*,' she wept. 'He was a bit like Heathcliff in those days and I just *adore* Heathcliff.'

'Ah,' I said. 'But Heathcliff's not a real person. He's a character in a book.'

'I know that,' she said, resuming her sobbing where she'd left off.

Excellent. At least she wasn't mad. I decided to try another approach. Change the subject. It's been known to work in extreme cases, particularly if the subject has a short attention span. I passed her another tissue.

'Know anything about Montserrat?' I said.

She looked at me for a long moment. 'You're Irish, aren't you?'

No point denying it twice – the soft Irish burr, remember? 'Yes,' I repeated. 'I am.'

She dabbed her eyes and gazed at me intently. 'Has

anyone ever told you you look like Leopold Bloom?'

'Not,' I replied nervously, 'as such.'

She was beginning to worry me now. The hero of the most celebrated if unread novel in all literature? What impressionable woman wouldn't want to sleep with him? I passed her the box of tissues and edged towards the door.

'And now,' I said, 'I really must be getting back.'

As I retreated, this possibly hormonal and patently delusional young woman pushed her chair back and stood up. 'Wait,' she squealed. I didn't. I made my way along the corridor at speed. She followed me, also at speed. 'No. Wait!' She grabbed me by the shoulders, pinned me to the wall and began sobbing loudly onto my jacket. 'Thank you,' she sobbed. 'Thank you thank you thank you.' I stood rigid with tension. Why rigid? Simple. What if Blaise chose this moment to emerge from the professor's study with the joyous news of her fellowship? She would find me in apparent flagrante with another woman. Was *this* the thing I'd done last time? Had I slept with an impressionable woman by posing as Leopold Bloom?

'You know what you have to do,' I said, disengaging and edging towards the drawing room door. Truth was, *I* didn't, so I hoped she wouldn't ask.

'I do?' she asked.

'Yes,' I said. 'You do.'

She braced herself.

'You're right,' she said, narrowing her eyes. 'I know *exactly* what I have to do.'

To my relief she turned briskly on her heel and made her way back down the corridor. As she reached the kitchen she turned. 'Thanks again, Leo,' she said. 'Truly.' Then she was gone.

I closed my eyes and took a deep breath. The incomprehensible conversations of the drawing room would be sweet relief after that little encounter. I opened the door and prepared to switch, mentally, off.

The place was in uproar. Bodies. Noise. Alcohol everywhere. Albertine belting out *The Fields of Boolavogue*. Professor Bridie in a green football shirt weeping into his drink. I'm not prepared to swear that a group of traditional musicians played in the corner and that a regiment of small girls in emerald dresses tapped out a jig on the drinks table, but they may as well have done. Did I conjure all this up simply by being Irish? Probably. You can rewrite your past but you can't escape it.

I was backing out the door when Albertine appeared from the midst of mayhem, grabbed me in a huge embrace – 'THERE'S MY LITTLE IRISHMAN!' – and yanked me into her amplitude. I was reminded of the chilling folk tale of Cúchulainn disappearing between Queen Maeve's breasts and never being seen again. Or perhaps I dreamed that one up. But here was I, about to disappear into Albertine's cavernous depths, when the door swung open and in came Blaise.

'I think we'd better leave,' was all she said.

Blaise was quiet as we headed for the car. As we got in. As she started the engine. I, too, was quiet. Whatever it was, I'd obviously done it. We were about to head off in mutual silence when a taxi pulled up outside the main door. The possibly-but-not-definitely mad young woman, without her canapés but now clutching a suitcase, rushed out and clambered in. The taxi door slammed shut as Professor Letchworth raced out after her, sporting a dishevelled goatee with matching black eye.

'CATH-Y!' he cried plaintively. 'CATH-Y!'

It was heartrending. Heartrending but futile. The taxi headed off at speed.

'Good for her,' muttered Blaise, as she drove through the main gate and headed, silent again, homewards. It was the sort of silence you couldn't interrupt, so I said nothing. Nothing on the journey home. Nothing as we went inside. Nothing as Blaise, her face a mask of sorrowful resolution, trudged dejectedly into her study. I felt terrible. The love of my life was experiencing the dark night of the soul and it was still only ten past nine.

I left her to it for several seconds, then braced myself. I was about to knock on the study door and launch into an extemporised speech of apology and self-abasement, when it opened of its own volition – no locks – and Blaise flew out. She threw her arms around me.

'I'm so, so sorry,' she said. 'I should never have put you through all that. I *knew* Professor Letchworth was a philandering bastard – '

'WHAT?!!!'

' – and when I intimated that I found him repulsive, you know what he said? That women aren't genetically programmed to write.' She suddenly brightened. 'You may have noticed his eye.'

'Indeed I did,' I said. 'His wife obviously socked him.'

'His wife? Oh, yeah. That'll be it,' said Blaise. Then

she moved closer in a come-hitherly sort of way. 'As for you,' she said, 'I'd like to thank you for not doing what you did last time. Although to be honest' – she stroked me seductively across the cheek – 'I wouldn't have minded if you had.'

Fecund

I put my knife and fork down slowly and leaned forward.

'No, Blaise,' I said. 'We are *not* having a baby.'

The whole restaurant fell silent.

'But I haven't said a word,' said Blaise.

'You were staring past me with that rapt look on your face,' I said. 'Is there, or is there not, a baby somewhere behind my right ear?'

Blaise now had that guilty look on her face. A fellow diner – male – decided to help me out. 'Baby at 30 degrees,' he said. I took him to be a nautical man and thanked him with a casual salute. His female companion tutted audibly. He'd become embroiled in the age old battle of the sexes, and he'd chosen the wrong side. I left them to their possibly disintegrating marriage and planned my next move. I didn't look around. I simply picked up my knife and fork, again slowly, and recommenced eating. I'd made my point. Masterfully. Or so I thought, until Blaise leaned forward.

'While we're on the subject of babies,' she whispered.

'Which we're not,' I said.

'But – ,' said Blaise. I stopped her right there. I knew her buts. This whole subject of babies had been up for discussion when we'd first co-habited. 'Think about it,' I'd said. 'If we have a child at my age I'll be – .' Then I had a better idea. 'Don't think about it.' Now here she was with that faraway look in her eye, that besotted gaze, that while-we're-on-the-subject schtick. No. I simply wasn't having it. I gave the old sea dog a second salute and almost poked an eye out with my fork.

And there the matter rested. But it had got me worried, so when we arrived home I headed straight for my well-thumbed copy of *Women's Bodies, Men's Wisdom*. It had never failed me yet. According to this excellent tome a man can be fecund well into his nineties. It recommended the *Are You Superfertile?* test and, not to be unnecessarily coy about it, I ticked all the boxes.

Blaise, on the other hand, I was relieved to read, was infertile. *Theoretically*.[6] A celebrated case in the Russian Steppes – documented in the book – involved a one hundred and twelve year old woman giving birth to triplets. With an accompanying photograph of the proud mother at a party to celebrate their combined 30th birthday. She put her late conception down to a diet of fresh air and buttermilk.

I checked the fridge just in case. I then used Blaise's immersion in creative work elsewhere to check her bedroom drawers and bathroom cupboards, looking for clues. I discovered a world I never knew existed. Blaise, a natural beauty, obviously believed in leaving nothing to chance. The cupboards were littered with eyebrow pencils, lipsticks and mascaras, bottles, phials and tubes. A tub which said, in clear gold lettering, *Merveilleux Pour Bébé*. I was immediately on high alert.

'What are you doing?' asked Blaise from the doorway. I almost jumped out of my trousers. But a lifetime of subterfuge – all for the greater good I hasten to add – has taught me that a ready answer, delivered with authority, works every time.

---

[6] My italics.

'I'm looking for condoms,' I said. Ah. That must have come from somewhere deep in the subconscious. I hadn't fully thought it through, but I was committed, so I prepared to stand my ground.

'Why?' asked Blaise. 'Thinking of having an affair?'

'That you should even ask,' I said. 'It's just that I appear to be superfertile, and I know what you're going to say. You're a woman. You've reached a certain age. You're *in*-fertile. But what if superfertile trumps infertile? Hadn't thought of that, had you?'

'I gave them to Bonnie,' said Blaise.

'Sorry?'

'The condoms. After we stopped using them. Bonnie was up. There was a packet left over.'

I was almost speechless. Bonnie, my beloved, if partially estranged, daughter, was – what – twelve?

'You gave. The condoms. To Bonnie.'

'Well I could hardly sell them, now could I? They were buy two get one free, remember? I gave her the free one.'

'I'm – I'm speechless,' I said.

'No you're not,' said Blaise. 'And I know exactly what you're going to say.'

'What can you possibly have been thinking?' I said. 'Bonnie is a mere child.'

'See? I was right. She's seventeen. She's in a relationship. I had my first relationship – '

'Stop it right there,' I said. 'I've rewritten history, and when I rewrite history it stays rewritten.'

Blaise was about to agree with me – we have an understanding on this point – when the phone rang. I left her to it and had another look at the tub. *Merveilleux Pour*

Bébé. Now I'm not a qualified linguist, but I'm willing to bet Bébé is French for Baby. What baby? There was no baby. At present. So why the tub? That's what *I* wanted to know. I was considering the question when I caught the end of Blaise's telephone conversation.

'This afternoon. See you then. Don't worry. Free all day. Come any time. Bye.'

Odd. There was something secretive about her tone, as if I might disapprove. This could mean only one thing. She put the phone down as I walked back into the living room. I steeled myself. 'Don't tell me,' I said.

Blaise opted for defiant. 'Okay then,' she said. 'I won't.' That sealed it, I'm afraid. It had to be her mother. Inviting herself for afternoon tea. I decided to meet her defiance head on.

'It's just that, well, I'm meeting Dan. I was going to bring him back. You know. Afternoon tea.'

'Slight complication,' said Blaise. 'It might be best if you stayed out for a while.'

On balance I tended to agree. Her mother had a personality that would freeze ice. Dan was my friend. I wanted to keep it that way.

Two hours later Dan and I were ensconced in *Little Italy* discussing
- Fertility. Effects of menopause on.
- Superfertility. Possible overriding effects of.

Dan feigned understanding and nodded wisely. 'How old is Blaise?' he asked, flicking the remnants of an *aragostine pistachio* from his moustache. I told him I wasn't prepared to discuss my wife's age in a public place but that she was, *theoretically*, past the childbearing threshold.

I then got on to the subject of *Merveilleux Pour Bébé*, finding of. I'd brought it with me. As evidence. Dan fingered it meditatively.

'Ah yes, well you see that's French,' he said. 'Bébé is French for Baby. I'd put money on it.'

I knew this, but it seemed to give him a certain standing in his own eyes and that was no bad thing. There is undoubtedly a crisis of masculinity abroad at present and every little helps. He puffed himself up.

'Yes,' he repeated. 'That's definitely French for Baby.' He leaned in closer. 'Re Blaise,' he said. 'I'd be happy to have a word.'

'You can't,' I said. 'She's entertaining her mother.'

'I see,' said Dan. 'How old is her mother?'

'Late eighties,' I said. 'Besides, she's not your type.'

Dan accepted this without question and we passed a very pleasant afternoon in idle chat, by which point Blaise's mother would have been a good three hours older and tucked up at home in bed. I invited Dan back for a quick bite and we arrived – as I later informed the police officer who took my statement – at precisely 4.15. No elderly mother. No Blaise. The only sign of life, in the middle of the table in the living room, was a baby asleep in a car seat[7].

Dan did a double take. 'That was quick,' he muttered.

'It's not ours,' I tried to hiss, but nothing came out of my mouth. I was in a state of shock, my mind a jumble of wild thoughts and images. How far was it to the Tiber? Did we have a wicker basket? I'd just decided that a car seat and the Clyde would do, when I heard the sound

---

[7] !!!

of typing from the study. Blaise had left the door ajar to keep an ear out for what was pretty patently a stolen child.

'We've got to get this baby out of here,' I hissed.

'Shouldn't we check with Blaise first,' Dan hissed back. 'There might be a perfectly good – '

'There's never a perfectly good reason for child theft. Blaise was broody, she saw her chance, she took it. I mean look at the little mite. He's – he's some mother's son, Dan.' I almost choked on this. I was some mother's son myself.

'Daughter,' said Dan. 'Observe the colour scheme. It's a dead giveaway.'

'Out,' I said. 'Now.'

Five minutes later we were hailing a taxi. We bundled in, baby first. The driver was one of those chatty types.

'Lovely to see the dads taking a hand,' he said. 'Where to?'

'The nearest police station,' I said.

The driver chortled the way taxi drivers do.

'Soiled its nappy, has it? Bit drastic.'

A cheap quip, I thought, and almost withheld the tip.

The desk sergeant was most solicitous. Babies scattered all over the place these days, he said. So where exactly had we found it?

'I'm afraid I can't tell you that,' I said, intending to protect my dearly beloved.

'Well, in that case I'm going to have to take down your particulars,' said the desk sergeant, possibly a mite frostily. 'Child theft is a very serious offence.'

'Don't be ridiculous, man,' I snapped. Which may have woken the child. At any rate, there it was – awake. Fortunately it was facing away from me at the time, so there was no bonding involved. It gurgled happily at the desk sergeant, who gurgled happily back.

'Leave this to me,' he said. He opened a drawer and placed a bag of nappies, a bottle, a tin of powdered milk and a packet of Farley's rusks on the counter. The child continued to gurgle. The desk sergeant turned his attention back to me.

'You were saying, Sir?'

'Was I?'

'*Don't be ridiculous, man.* Quote unquote.'

'Ah yes. We didn't steal the child. It was – '

I stopped there. I simply couldn't do it. Blaise would probably thrive in a women's prison and have all the inmates writing poetry, but still.

'Well, Sir?'

'It was person or persons unknown,' I said, my voice slightly less sure of itself this time.

'Bit vague, Sir,' said the desk sergeant, absently nibbling a rusk. 'Which puts you right back in the frame.'

'In that case,' I said, 'I believe we're entitled to a free phone call.'

'Fair enough, Sir,' said the desk sergeant, 'but I pity the recipient.'

Interesting point. The recipient. I could hardly phone Blaise. She was the problem, not the solution. Who, then? A good lawyer? I didn't know any. A man of the cloth? Not after last time. I was casting my mental net wider when Dan cut in.

'Okay if I make the call?' he said.

'All the same to me,' said the desk sergeant. I was stuck at Not Blaise so I shrugged my agreement. The desk sergeant plonked a phone on the counter and motioned Dan on.

He dialled the number and waited. Which gave me an opportunity to study him in depth. Dan was tall, with a shock of white hair and a long, lugubrious face. This was offset by a long, lugubrious moustache. People referred to him affectionately as Dan Quixote, which suited him in an odd sort of way. No windmills, no lance, no horse. But otherwise.

'Is that Ibrahim?' he said. A brief pause. 'Dan here. I've got an appointment for ten tomorrow. Looks like I'll have to cancel.' Another pause. 'Hold on. I'll check.' Dan lowered the phone and addressed the desk sergeant. 'Any idea how long we're likely to be detained for this particular misdemeanour?' he said.

'Hardly a misdemeanour, Sir,' said the desk sergeant. 'Child theft is a very serious crime.'

'Right so,' said Dan. 'Could you maybe give me an approx.'

The desk sergeant fingered his rusk meditatively and thought about this for a long moment. 'Well, Sir,' he said, 'we stopped it before it got out of hand so no harm done. Looks good on the statistics, but that's by the by. So let me see now. I'd say six years max. You look the good behaviour type' – he shot me a look; let's call it pointed – 'so possibly open prison. Out in three? depends on the judge but call that an informed guess.'

Dan went back on the phone.

'Ib? Have you got your diary for 2017?' A short pause. 'Nov 3rd sounds great. 2.30? Magic. See you then.' He lowered the phone. 'Turkish barbers. Three fifty for a cut and shave, but worth every penny.' He lowered his voice. 'They set fire to your ears. I love that bit.' He put the phone back. It rang immediately. 'Hold on,' said Dan. 'Probably a date cock up.' He answered. 'Ibrahim?' Another pause. 'Blaise. Good to – oh, right. I'll put him on.' He held the phone out to the desk sergeant. 'It's for you.'

I could hear Blaise talking animatedly on the other end of the line. The desk sergeant listened politely.

'He's here all right,' he said. 'And so is the baby.'

Blaise arrived ten minutes later. She told the desk sergeant it had all been a terrible misunderstanding and he agreed that we – the accused – could be released into her care pending further enquiries. This was *way* off the mark as far as the cold, hard facts were concerned, but I kept my own counsel. We left him eyeing the rusk packet surreptitiously.

Dan wandered off to renegotiate his appointment with the Turkish barbers while Blaise and I took a taxi home. Which gave me time to think. To reason with Blaise. To negotiate the return of this baby to its rightful mother. This might prove difficult. It now nestled peacefully in Blaise's arms, which worried me more than slightly.

'Lucky for you Mandy was held up at the dentist,' said Blaise after what seemed like a long pause.

'Mandy?' I said.

'Nancy's mum,' said Blaise.

This was serious. She knew the mother's identity and movements. She also appeared to have named the child. Her little escapade had been carefully choreographed down to the last detail.

'So what are you planning to do with – this?'

I pointed vaguely at the child.

'Why, return her to Mandy,' said Blaise.

I should think so too, I thought. You should never have taken it in the first place. But I said nothing. I would just keep an extra eye on her over the weeks and months ahead. It was hopefully just a phase.

War and the Menopause

Blaise had been jumpy all day. Anxious. Irritable. No apparent reason. Probably hormonal, I thought. So I decided to refer to my bible on the subject – *Women's Bodies Men's Wisdom*. Pretty soon I was drawn into some of the murkier areas of this once forbidden field of research.

Take, for instance, the following. 'A stiletto in the forehead suggests possible menopausal behaviour. Before removing make sure shoe not still on foot as it may aggravate subject further.'

Chilling stuff, but Blaise, fortunately, was just at the thinking-about-it stage.

Things, however, were about to get a whole lot worse.

I awoke that night to find a figure at the end of my bed. Ghost? Burglar? Not so. It was *Menopausal Woman* with a slightly mad glint in her eye.

'I've just finished my war poem,' she said. I was stunned, and as soon as she'd fallen asleep I superglued the cutlery drawer and hid her stilettos. I then fell into a deep and troubled sleep, and dreamed a deep and troubled dream. Blaise as Boudica. Horned helmet. Full red beard. This I could take. But she also sat in a very unladylike way.

Morning confirmed the worst.

'You haven't forgotten the war demo?' she said, as she demolished her muesli. 'We're off to Edinburgh[8] in five minutes.'

---

[8] Beautiful city. Often referred to, I believe, as the Glasgow of the North.

War *demo*? A war poem was bad enough, but actually touting for business? I began to look on Blaise with fresh eyes. This was positively bloodthirsty behaviour. Yet my unease faded in the face of her great beauty. A warmonger she may have been, but she was damned attractive with it.

While she put her face on – her words – I decided to step outside. I was dealing here with a menopausal time-bomb. The fact that I'd made it this far without a 4-inch heel in the cranium was no mean achievement, so I slid into the passenger seat and pondered my options. War? I wasn't really in favour. I had to find some way of bringing the subject up delicately – without precipitating a hormonal crisis.

It wasn't until the traffic on the motorway had begun to snarl up that I saw my chance. Blaise eased her foot off the accelerator and rummaged in her fruit bag. My idea this. A constant supply of fresh produce reduced the subject of her weight from an hourly to a daily complaint. She plucked a Cox's Pippin from the bag, and was about to ease the car to a halt, when an enormous 4-wheel drive nipped into the few remaining feet in front. Blaise braked hard and almost pulped her fruit.

'Blaise,' I said gently, 'I hope this doesn't affect our wonderfully loving relationship in any way, but about this war demo – I'm not actually the warmongering type.'

Before I could get to the bit about much preferring peace, she'd slammed the door shut behind her and was banging furiously on the blacked-out window of the monstrosity in front. No response. She reached up and banged again. Nothing. Blaise internalised her rage, which had the odd effect of making her hair boil. She strode to the rear of the offending vehicle, shoved her pippin up the exhaust pipe – which I'm not sure is strictly legal – and returned, seething, to her seat.

'What?' she seethed, rummaging in her fruit bag for a replacement.

'Sorry?' I said.

'You were saying.'

I decided to get straight to the point.

'War,' I paraphrased. 'You for. Me against.'

She gave me one of her pitying looks.

'Me against too,' she said. 'Why do you think we're going on the demo?'

At which point the traffic started moving. Well, except for the monstrosity in front. All four doors opened, smoke billowed out, and a nuclear family hopped down to the street below. Blaise switched lanes and moved on. Her hair went off the boil. She settled back and sighed happily.

Happy that the traffic was moving again.

Or happy, perhaps, with the sugar rush from her chocolate orange.

I felt reassured. Blaise hummed happily as she demolished segment after segment of brown fruit. We were at one on the war front, so I was now happy. It was, therefore, a happy car that approached the city centre, bouncing along on its ancient suspension.

I had entered that dreamy state where thoughts of making love mingled with thoughts of banishing war, forever, from the face of this sad planet, when I heard Blaise's voice as if from afar.

'I said *out*!'

'Sorry?'

The car had pulled over. The traffic lights were red. Her hair was simmering again. 'I'm reading the poem, remember? To 50,000 people. You'll have to forgive me if I'm a little jumpy. So hop out, join the march, and I'll see you later.'

'Hold on,' I said. 'Relax.' Wrong word. The lights were still red. So was she.

'I've got to do a sound-check. I need the toilet. Good Bye.'

I opened the door, looked at her and saw, for an instant, the little girl she once was – well, presumably – and my heart fluttered with love. I placed a soothing hand on her shoulder. 'The psychology of performance,' I said, 'is very simple.'

'Get out,' she said. 'Now. Before I kill you.'

I rummaged in her bag and produced a Curly Wurly. Which is not, strictly speaking, a member of the fruit family. '50,000 people,' I said, passing it over. 'A pretty frightening number. But let's say you could boil them down to one.' I could tell by the way she gnawed her Curly Wurly that she was still jumpy. 'Best take the wrapper off first,' I advised. 'Okay. Here's the plan. I'll stand smack dab in the middle of the audience. Read the poem,' I soothed, 'just for me.'

The sound of car horns woke us from our reverie. I jumped out. The lights turned back to red. Blaise drove off. I watched as she gestured to a line of irate motorists and marvelled, yet again, at her beauty. We would make love later, but first there was the small matter of the war.

As I approached the meeting point for the protest I surveyed my fellow demonstrators and spotted, among the ranks, the family from the enormous car. Mother. Father. Two little boys. I felt I knew them in a funny sort of way, so I sauntered over and fell in step nearby.

The boys, I noted, held banners aloft with pride.

NOT IN MY NAME

NOT IN MY NAME EITHER

Heartwarming stuff - or so I thought. Until, that is, they started whacking each other over the heads with the damn things. The parents? Totally oblivious. They danced on ahead blowing peace bubbles in a fey manner and smiling beatifically.

Which put me in a pretty interesting position. In bygone days I would have given both boys a sound thrashing and thought no more about it. But these are not bygone days, and won't be for some time to come, so the sound thrashing scenario was not an option.

The situation had deteriorated by this stage. The banners were now shattered beyond repair, the splintered handles an acceptable substitute for broadswords. The boys had embraced the delirium of battle. And the parents? Just a sporadic burst of bubbles up ahead.

Enough dithering. The time had come for action. 'Right,' I barked. 'That's it! Both of you to your rooms! This instant!'

Whatever the reason – their subconscious desire for the imposition of strict parameters is *my* guess – it worked. They lowered their broadswords sheepishly and slunk off and, as I watched their neatly creased little shorts disappearing in the distance I felt immensely gratified. I had been firm of purpose and it had patently worked.

On the rest of us marched and there, you'd be forgiven for thinking, the matter rested; sighs of relief all round. Not a bit of it. The first sign that all wasn't well was the absence of bubbles. They'd been pretty constant and, to be honest, faintly irritating, but suddenly they simply ceased to be. The plaintive cries which replaced them, however, were pretty grating.

'Justin!'

'Julian!'

Good names. They went with the shorts. But as with most things shouted ad nauseum the novelty soon wore off, and constant repetition became, instead, a tedious mantra.

I wasn't, however, entirely unsympathetic. It's pretty tough being a parent these days. And I soon made them out jostling with their fellow marchers as they fell back in the ranks and yelled in vain for their missing boys. I was more than happy to put their minds at ease, and moved forward to meet them half way.

'I've sent them to their rooms,' I said, linking arms and easing them back into line.

Dad was the first to speak.

'But – but we live in Tuscany.'

'I'm delighted to hear it,' I said. 'I believe it's particularly lovely at this time of year.'

'That's hardly the point,' he spluttered. 'Tuscany is twelve hundred miles away.'

'And?'

'If you send a child to its room,' snapped Mum, who seemed the emotional sort, 'it sort of helps if you're at home.'

'Ah,' I said. 'Take your point.' I was in danger of losing their sympathy, but rallied quickly. 'Still, look on the bright side. If the lads take their time, you might miss out on those difficult teenage years. Just a thought.'

Mum was outraged.

'You – you despicable man.'

'Now now, darling,' protested Dad. 'He's pretty spot-on there. Teenage boys? Bloody nightmare.'

Mum turned her attention to Dad.

'That's it, isn't it?' she spat. 'You never actually wanted them in the first place.'

'Well, now you mention it,' he replied evenly. 'No. I didn't. Simple as that.'

Mum narrowed her already pursed lips.

'In that case,' she sneered venomously, 'I've got some *excellent* news. You're not the real father.'

I was astounded! And Dad? He was so upset by this body blow to his manhood that he almost fell out of step.

'Not – their real father?'

I tried to reassure him. 'Statistically, apparently, very few people are.' But before I could give him the precise figures, I was interrupted by a police officer, and to be honest I welcomed the intrusion. Justin and Julian had done what they were told. End of story. I'd tried to placate the parents, but I knew the sort. They'd keep harping on about it ad infinitum given the chance. No. The time had come to draw a line under the incident and move on.

Which is why I welcomed the officer. He'd just

recognised Mum. Hadn't seen her for the best part of ten years. He was also, I would have to say, the spitting image of Justin. Also possibly Julian. Dad noted the likeness too. I *say* Dad, but in the light of Mum's little revelation I wondered if he had another name.

Not the best time to ask, though, as he'd just grabbed hold of the policeman. Another policeman retaliated – isn't it always the way! – and several burly protesters joined in. Suddenly the peace march was mayhem, with fists flying everywhere, horses trampling the casual onlookers, barricades erected, helicopters whirring overhead, Mum and Dad slugging it out on opposite sides, while I, my pacifist credentials intact, was left holding the bubbles. I managed to slip away from the extremely fraught proceedings, and duck down a side street, as an elite squad of paratroopers arrived to cordon off the riot.

I rediscovered the route of the march and continued on my way, a lone voice against the obscenity of war, accompanied only by the sword of truth and the fragile bubbles of peace. But from tiny bubbles, as the ancient saying has it, do mighty bubbles grow. Empowered by this thought, I turned the corner to my final destination some minutes later. There before me lay a broad expanse of lush, rolling green, a huge stage looming up in the distance. I marched proudly to the middle and stood there, a solitary figure, clutching the bubbles of peace and facing the front of the stage. Moments later, Blaise strode confidently from the wings, grabbed the mike and, all trace of nervousness gone, read her poem.

Just, as I'd suggested, for me.

As we drove home Blaise popped brown grapes into her mouth from a bag marked *Maltesers*. She was happy, I was happy, and, as a huge 4-wheel drive with blacked out windows nipped in front of us during the inevitable snarl up, I peeled a chocolate orange and handed it to Blaise. 'For the exhaust.'

Blaise looked at the exhaust. Then she looked at the orange. She smiled enigmatically, smashed the chocolate orange into segments on the dashboard, and popped one into her mouth.

Peace at last.

Salmon Chamareemo

A major coup for Blaise's writing group. A.L. Kennedy had agreed to come and read. Prestigious venue. Great interest. This, apparently, was fan*tast*ic news. I was delegated to collect the legendary author from the station. Trouble was, I hadn't a clue what he looked like.

I was pondering this problem as the 18.41 pulled in. Perhaps I should phone Blaise and admit this gap in my knowledge. Not possible, unfortunately. I'd waxed lyrical on the subject that very day. Superb talent. Huge fan. That sort of thing. Perhaps, I ventured, our greatest living writer. I felt safe in assuming he *was* a writer. The living bit too seemed a pretty good bet. But these were my only clues, and the train had just sighed to a halt.

The brain works fast in these situations. What does an author look like? I was no great expert on the subject, but it seemed likely, at the very least, that he'd be drunk. Hemingway. Behan. The little Welsh chap. It wasn't much to go on, but most of the passengers strode past me towards the exit. All I had to do was wait for the drunk who didn't.

The crowd dispersed. Odd. All that remained was a lone woman. Bit of a mature student look. She stood there, possibly waiting for her boyfriend, while I tut-tutted, examined my watch, fingered the cavernous wastelands of my trouser pockets; the outward signs of exasperation. The woman looked agitated, paced around for a while, began rooting through her bag. A book cover surfaced in the jumble.

Now this was uncanny. The book was by none other than A.L. Kennedy himself. What a stroke of luck. I was about to ask if she had any idea what he looked like when the train doors were prised open from the inside and a large man staggered blinking into the sunlight, hat askew, shirt tails out, the contents of his briefcase tumbling earthward. Singing *Salmon Chamareemo*[9] at the top of his voice. Now that's what I call a writer.

I hurried over and helped him retrieve his notes. Let me rephrase that. I hurried over and retrieved his notes. *He* decided to relieve himself onto the track. He fumbled beneath the generous folds of his stomach, but was unable to locate his trousers. He then abandoned plan A and decided to light the tip end of a cigarette instead. This attention to the minutiae of the writer's persona marked him down as the genuine article. I'd obviously found my man.

I waved the collected papers under his nose and made for the exit. He followed me, like a very large two-year-old, out of the station. I'd been right about the drink, as I knew I would be. All I had to do now was keep him away from prostitutes and brawls. At least until I'd got him to the venue.

The journey from station to venue was fraught with peril. I managed to pour him into the last remaining taxi, but he positively cascaded out the other side. They'd left the child lock off. He tried several times to pay for the journey, by which time the woman had given up on her boyfriend and commandeered the taxi. I couldn't help feeling that a walk and a good cry might have suited her better in the circumstances. Added to which, she must

---

[9] The song, not the Mediterranean fish starter.

have been aware of who Al was, and could so easily have shown deference to his genius. But such is the modern world.

So we walked. We visited several bars en route – and here's a curious thing: the bar staff in all six obviously knew him but referred to him throughout as Frank. Wily ruse this. The alias. Anonymity. Very important for a writer.

I also humoured him on the brothel front. I had no choice in the matter, to be honest. He literally dragged me there. I must say, though, as brothels go it was very discreet. To the untrained eye a typical West End terrace. Well-trimmed hedge. Volvo. There were even a few kids dotted about to fool the authorities. The madam, a homely woman with a child under each arm, seemed consumed by rage as she hurled insult after insult at poor old Al, who was trying to urinate against the cotoneaster. Writers and prostitutes! An explosive mix.

I got the distinct impression, after the door had been slammed and double bolted, that Al was persona non grata in that particular establishment and that sexual gratification was out of the question. On that occasion at least.

The half mile journey between brothel and venue passed without further incident, if we exclude a brief tango with a post box. He also attempted to serenade a woman whose name was *not* Delilah and woo a florist with her own flowers. Invoice to follow.

Some time later we negotiated the automatic doors of the venue. After a fashion. As I staggered through the foyer with Al declaring his undying love and promising 'to take me away from all this', I noticed that Blaise was deep in conversation with a woman. Bit of a mature student look. She seemed vaguely familiar, but I was too busy trying to get Al's orchids out of my face to give it much thought.

I finally managed to prop him up at the bar, and left him there, happily slurring at the bar staff and trying to stuff his mangled bouquet in someone else's pint. And get this. As I was leaving, a barman said 'Still at the bank, Frank?' Good old Al. What a guy. Not only the false name, but a false profession to boot. He was well covered on the privacy front.

The foyer, by the time I got back to it, was empty. The audience had taken their seats. But what about the star attraction? I noticed a table of his books taking pride of place in the centre of the room. Tons of the things. I wondered where he found time to write 'em, to be honest. But there, at any rate, they were.

I brushed past them into the auditorium. The lights were down on the audience. I peered into the darkness but couldn't see a thing.

'Blaise,' I hissed. 'Are you in there?'

'I'm in the middle of a haiku,' she replied. 'And I'm over here.' I finally made her out, fully spotlit, behind the microphone.

'So you are,' I said. 'Do go on.'

She began to explain, to murmurs of approval from the audience, that it was very difficult to read a haiku in two parts. Why? I didn't catch that bit. I'd just noticed something which chilled the hairs on the back of my neck. Pacing in the shadows offstage, rigid with concentration, was the vaguely familiar woman.

What on earth was she up to? She must have followed us here. Granted, she got here first, but this was probably just a subtle way of covering her tracks. She had then inveigled herself into Blaise's confidence. Now here she was, looking for her footnote in history. There was no way the great man was going on that stage. I could see the headlines now.

'Kennedy Shooting: Woman Held.'

I rushed out of the auditorium without a single thought for my own personal safety.

Into the bar. No Al.

'Where's Al?'

'Who's Al?'

I said nothing. *I* wasn't going to blow his cover.

I rushed back out. Where could he possibly be? The gents. I rushed in. Two Jeremys. One Murdoch. A man who refused to give his name without a warrant.

I rushed out. Pandemonium. What sounded like a prison riot. Coming straight from the ladies. I had obviously found my man. Again. Then I remembered the not-so-small matter of the stalker. First things first. I rushed over to the box office.

'I think you'd better call the police,' I panted.

'We already have.'

'Excellent work. You spotted her too.'

I rushed back into the auditorium.

But what's this?

The would-be-assassin was standing onstage. Reading from one of Al's books if you please. The audience? The audience was rapt. *Rapt!* Mass hypnosis? I'm no expert, but I knew one thing: I had to get Al out of here. It was nothing less than a madhouse.

When I returned to the foyer a troupe of women was filing out of the ladies. Cackling. Bad sign. I waited till the cackling had died off in the distance and made my way, very tentatively, inside. I knew the risks, but I needn't have worried. In the middle of the floor of the ladies, everything askew and smiling beatifically, sat Scotland's greatest living author.

I was in the act of hoicking him on to a lavatory seat when a police officer came in. Followed by – difficult to believe but it was that sort of evening – the madam. No kids – and she was speechless with rage.

The officer spoke for both of them.

'Come along then, Frank,' he said. 'Time for beddy-byes.'

So that was it. The poor woman was being forced to accept an unwanted client by a bent cop. My attempt to remonstrate on her behalf was met by a slap across the face. Which I accepted with good grace. As Al staggered out of the ladies with his pathetic entourage I looked on with a strange mix of admiration and yet, somehow, moral revulsion.

Drink. Prostitutes. Brawls. I found myself wondering if writers indulge in this sort of carry on for pleasure or research when I was interrupted in my reverie by the excited babble of female voices. 'Scotland's greatest living etc.' That sort of thing. They'd obviously met Al in the foyer. They seemed less thrilled to see *me* – loitering with intent, they called it - so I indulged in a symbolic hand wash, mumbled something about the Kennedy shooting, and left.

The foyer was packed. An enormous queue wound in ever increasing circles up to the table. Our stalker?

Holding court at the self same table. Twirling a biro as if she owned the thing. Gaily defacing copies of Al's life's work.

I was mulling this over in bed that night when Blaise said something which stunned me to the very core of my beliefs.

'The less said about a certain matter the better,' she said, 'but I thought A.L. was fan*tast*ic tonight.'

I'm none the wiser to this day as to what the certain matter might have been, but no, I thought. Al was *not* fantastic. Al was an insult to a noble calling. Blaise, it seems, had bought straight into the notion of the great writer as male, boorish and drunk. Time, perhaps, to consign that hoary old cliché to the reference library of history.

I said nothing – the situation with Blaise seemed a trifle delicate at that point – but I did entertain a rather odd thought. In a funny sort of way the stalker – deranged, no doubt, but not obviously armed, unless we include the casually twirled pen – had probably saved the night.

Better all round, perhaps, if the great man himself had been a woman.

Are Women Funny?

I hadn't seen my beloved daughter, Bonnie, for some time. Her mother, as I recall, was still acting in loco parentis. Touchy subject. So I was delighted when Blaise told me that Bonnie was travelling up from London that very day and would be staying over.

'She obviously misses her daddy,' I said. 'The bonds of blood and so forth.'

'Well,' said Blaise, 'there *is* that possibility. But it's not quite how she explained it to *me*.'

'She wouldn't,' I said. 'Would she? I mean when *I* was twelve – .'

Blaise patted me gently. The pity pat.

'Bonnie is seventeen,' she said. 'Got that? It's very important.'

'Got it,' I said. 'So why did she say she was coming up?'

'She's at drama college, remember?'

'Really?' I said. 'Isn't she a bit – '

'No she isn't,' said Blaise. 'She's seventeen. Anyway, she's chosen a standup comedy module. They've got to do twenty minutes somewhere out their comfort zone. So she's chosen Glasgow University Students Union.' Blaise looked dubious. 'Bit Neanderthal to be honest, but I suppose that's part of the deal.'

I was immediately thrown into protective Superdad mode. My lovely daughter at the mercy of a hall-full of boorish louts? I could almost feel the primary-coloured underpants outside my trousers.

'Perhaps I can help her,' I said.

'Please don't,' said Blaise. 'Please-please-please.' She held me close for a long moment. 'Please.'

Put like that it was hard to refuse, but Blaise wasn't happy till I'd signed a binding commitment to that effect, double witnessed by herself using her real name and the name she uses for her children's books.

'What children's books?' I said.

'Never mind about that now,' she said. 'This is serious.'

It certainly was. To be honest, I see comedy as a phase young people go through before the real business of existence kicks in. Life is more tragedy with little pockets of light relief at my age. I decided to do a bit of research on the computer, mainly to put my mind at ease. There probably wasn't anything to worry about. But wait for this. I put the word comedy into the search engine. Of 247,132,446 results in .34 of a second, the first entry asked simply *'Are Women Funny?'*

According to the piece in question a panel of experts had been lined up to address that very question. Verdict? Some of the experts suggested that women *were* funny. The other experts, and they seemed evenly divided on this, were of the opinion that they *weren't*. One expert, in the cause of evenhandedness, suggested that women who were funny *were* funny, which left the women who weren't. These, argued the expert, *weren't*. Simple as that. A further point was made that men were often unintentionally funny, which was seen by some as cheating. I was no closer to finding a definitive answer, so I trawled the comments.

This was a positive minefield. The level of debate

was potentially explosive, and it was still running at fifty-fifty. I decided to give the casting vote to the final comment. Whatever it was. I had to read this more than once to make sure I'd got it right. *'My story is that I quit Walmart to work online and with a little efortt I easily bring in at leaste $40h working from home.'* I stopped reading at this point. Difficult to know how it moved the discussion on.

Which brought me back to Bonnie and her student union gig. It was a war zone out there. She would need all the help she could get. I steeled myself and broke the news to Blaise that night at dinner. 'I'm going in,' I said.

I'd unwittingly used a military metaphor, but that was how I felt. Blaise knew exactly what I meant. Perhaps it was the set of my jaw. The steely gaze. The imaginary grenade. She knew when not to argue.

'Go,' she said, 'if go you must. But promise not to show your face.' She was about to hold me tight and go down the 'please' route again. I can always tell.

'Okay,' I interrupted, 'but I'm signing nothing. Whatever happened to trust?'

I left the flat a short time later and decided to walk. I won't bore you with details of the trip. There was a small incident involving me, an open manhole and a carelessly discarded banana skin, which seemed to amuse a passing coach-load of squaddies, but the lower echelons of the armed forces are not noted for their sophistication, so I clambered out, wiped a toxic substance from my trousers and walked on[10].

A short stroll past some of the university's historic

---

[10] The episode has since attracted a large internet following, but we won't go into that.

buildings brought me to the door of the student union bar. It was one of those low dives best left undescribed, and I was greeted with suspicion by the burly youth on the door. No, I insisted, I hadn't got the wrong venue. I had a personal interest in one of the acts. Thank *you*. I was also treated with what might have been sneering servility at the bar, when I ordered a bottle of their finest spring water.

'Make it sparkling,' I quipped. 'It's been quite a day.'

The place was packed. I pushed through the crowd and positioned myself by the back wall. I'd promised Blaise I'd stay out of sight and there was a convenient pillar nearby. I leaned against it and took a swig of my drink. The sparkles hit the roof of my mouth but failed to soothe my frazzled nerves. My little girl was about to stand up in front of at least two hundred of her contemporaries, many of them male. I knew what they were like. I used to be one myself. I took another swig as the lights went down and a lone spot lit the stage.

I hardly remember the entertainment early on. The compère. An act. The compère again. That sort of thing. To be honest, I was thinking about Bonnie through the ages. Grazing her knee. Falling off her bike. Losing her first tooth. I must have been totally lost in this nostalgia-fest because next time I looked at the stage who was there but Bonnie holding the microphone, bathed in a solitary spot. I finished my drink and may have swallowed the bottle.

'Actually,' said Bonnie, 'my dad lives in Glasgow.' The crowd cheered. 'Now you know that Oedippy stuff about killing your father and sleeping with your mother. I mean, it's supposed to be a boy thing. But hey, no-one told *me*!' The crowd whooped. 'Seriously though, I didn't murder old Pater. Just winged him.' The crowd hooted. Interesting. She'd invented a fictional father and the audience seemed to like him. 'So after he split with Mum he introduced me to his new girlfriend. I thought you'd get on, he said. I mean, she's in your class.' The crowd went wild.

I was beginning to relax. Her stage father was a well-drawn character. I felt I had a nice mental image. Bit of a rogue but lovable. She'd just got to the bit where she sends him a Father's Day card addressed to The Sperm Donor,[11] when a young drunk in front of me cupped his hands over his mouth.

'Speaking of sperm, sweetheart,' he roared, 'I'd nail you any time.'

Nail you? Nail you?! What on earth did he mean? I was about to ask him just that when Bonnie shot back.

'Nail?' she said. 'You flatter yourself, pal. I've seen it. More like a carpet tack.' The audience roared its approval. Then it hit me. This nail, as in *'I'd nail you any time'*, was nothing less than a veiled reference to –

I couldn't finish the sentence. I was furious. By this stage I was up at the bar. I wasn't having this. This was my daughter he was besmirching with his vile talk of –

I couldn't finish that sentence either.

'Give me two jugs of your finest cheap lager,' I hissed at the bar boy. 'No need for a glass.' He looked at me with a new respect. I paid for them just as the odious young heckler struck again.

'Show us your tits, darlin'.'

This was – this was outrageous. Tits?!

---

[11] Funny, I'd got one of those too.

'Why?' said Bonnie. 'Still on the breast at your age?'

The audience roared. Again.

He flumped back in his seat, defeated, but I was incandescent. Tits?!! I poured both jugs over his head. The audience erupted. I was grabbed on both sides by a couple of burly students in what may have been rugby shirts and bundled quickly out. My parting shot – 'Tits?!!!' – seemed to test their combined intellects. I'd obviously been right about the shirts.

I won't bore you with details of the trip home. I overheard a few snippets of passing conversation. 'Leave him alone, I think he's got Tourettes.' 'I don't think he's referring to yours, Mum.' That sort of thing. I strode home fuelled by rage. Blaise was getting ready for bed when I finally got in. Still seething. She wanted to know where I got my black eye. So I told her. I'd probably blown it with Bonnie for several more years, but I wasn't having my little girl treated as – as –

'A sex object?' said Blaise as she dabbed me with something wet.

I smouldered but said nothing.

'She's not your little girl,' said Blaise. 'You've got to let her grow up.' She kissed me on top of the head. 'Time for bed. We'll build bridges in the morning.'

Blaise had just gone to the bathroom when the front doorbell rang. She rushed back out.

'I'll get it,' she said. 'Maybe you should, you know – ', and she gestured towards the bedroom.

I sat where I was. Bonnie could be pretty explosive – she learned to stamp her tiny foot in the cradle – so it was better, on balance, to get it over with. Blaise opened the door. Bonnie burst in.

'Unbelievable!' she shrieked. 'I mean, that was literally unbe*lie*vable!'

I braced myself. She plonked her bag on the table and sat down facing me. 'I was doing fine, right? So Jake – he's in year three – he's supposed to shout stuff up. You know, try to throw me. Only he's a bit of a tosser old Jake, so he goes *way* too far. Stuff about – well, let's not go there. So this old guy lays into him.' She hugged her knees and giggled. 'My hero. Didn't see a thing myself. I mean *those lights*. So the old guy gets chucked out, poor sod. Anyway, Jake had to take an early shower, I got a standing ovation and three paid gigs. Bloody hell. What happened to your eye?'

'He banged into a cupboard,' said Blaise. 'He's not used to the kitchen.'

Not true. I've actually been in there several times, but I decided to let it pass.

'So,' I said. 'This – *hero* of yours. Sounds like a pretty amazing guy.'

'I was well impressed,' said Bonnie. 'Pity they chucked him out. I mean, I would've liked – '

'Anyway,' said Blaise, 'it's probably as well they did.' She looked across at me. 'On balance.'

I was about to disagree with Blaise on this. 'But why – ' I began.

Blaise kicked me under the table and turned to Bonnie. 'You look done in,' she said. 'All that travel and your performance. Well done, by the way. Sounds like you really delivered.' Bonnie yawned thanks. 'Tell you what,' said Blaise. 'Why don't you use the bathroom first. You're in the spare room. We'll see you in the morning.'

She motioned me towards the bedroom. But I didn't

feel like bed. I, too, was tripping. It had been quite an evening. So I told Blaise I'd follow her in – she shrugged her on-your-head-be-it shrug – and I sat on the sofa and opened the laptop. *Are Women Funny?* There were now 4,237 comments. One man said – and I thought this was pretty significant – his great aunt Eileen had been hilarious in a deadpan way but had found it impossible to get a breakthrough in the comedy clubs of the day. Until, that is, she changed her name to Les Dawson.

There, I thought, was the problem in a nutshell. Or was it? Another three comments had just come in. I was about to find out what they had to add to this most complex of subjects when Bonnie came out of the bathroom. I pretended I was glued to the screen. I heard her crossing the room, sensed her standing behind me, felt her staring at the back of my head.

'They say the best training for an artistic career is a screwed-up childhood,' she said, leaning over to peck me on the cheek. 'Thanks, Dad.'

Then she was gone. I sat there for some minutes. Several new comments blurred the screen in front of me. I wiped my eyes, closed the computer and went into the bedroom. Blaise peered at me over her reading glasses. I slipped in beside her and lay for a long moment.

'Bonnie kissed me,' I said. 'Let the healing begin.'

Bottled Air

Blaise delivered her instructions as if to a half-wit. The poem on the kitchen table, she said. Could I place it in the envelope marked Women's Poetry Competition. Could I hand deliver it to Television House. Could I do this by mid-day at the latest. She then counted the instructions off on her fingers. Poem into envelope. Deliver envelope. Mid-day deadline. One two three. If the poem won, she assured me, we'd be able to pay the mortgage arrears. Blaise rounded off her little speech with something about the bailiffs, then looked at me in a stern but not unloving way. 'Never mind,' she said. 'I'll do it myself.'

At which point the phone rang.

'You're stuck where?' said Blaise. 'I'll be right over.'

This would be, and was, Blaise's mother, a woman who had long since entered that twilight world of the aged where fantasy and reality meet and jostle with tragicomic results. On this occasion she'd bought a tree surgeon's harness on ebay and she was stuck. Not halfway up, she insisted, but halfway down, which meant it was back to plan A on the deadline front. One two three. Bye now. With that Blaise drove off and left me to it.

I picked up the poem in question. Frankly, it didn't make a great deal of sense. It mentioned milk, oatmeal, Tunnocks tea cakes and broccoli in no particular order. But then, poetry is not my strong suit. The final line – *Bottle of wine – no, best make that a crate!* – stood out in forming a sentence of sorts, but it didn't rhyme with the previous line – '*Oranges*' – so no consolation there for the traditionalists.

To be honest I wasn't convinced of its chances of winning, and the subject matter suggested that she was ill-advised to write on an empty stomach. But I had made my promise and would carry it out to the letter.

'Sorry I'm late,' I panted to the harassed receptionist at Television House as I plopped the envelope onto her desk.

Just then an earnest looking woman with a clipboard strode towards me. 'Never mind about that now,' she said. 'Follow me.'

I was ushered through a series of doors and marched along a series of corridors until we finally entered a room full of people, all seated in a semi-circle, facing a steely-eyed man flanked by a couple of flunkeys. I was frogmarched to the last empty chair. The lighting was distributed evenly around the room, yet it seemed drawn to this craggy-faced, square-jawed, pugnacious-looking individual with the fist-gripped waistcoat and well-chomped Corona.

'Above all,' he rasped, fixing me with both eyes in a pincer movement, 'Sir Roger Gravelle doesn't like late. Late has no place here. Late,' he barked, 'is for sissies.'

My age dropped several decades, my trousers shortened to match, and my mind returned, unbidden, to the final blow-out with my father. 'Begone,' he'd thundered. 'Stand not upon the order of your going, but go now.' And here was this man barking as my father had barked, rasping as my father had rasped, and all with the steely gaze of Patriarchal Man.

'Sorry Dad,' I almost said, and blushed prettily in the almost saying.

Sir Roger looked away. Pity? Contempt? Difficult to tell, but my short trousers remained. I was in thrall to this charismatic figure and would follow him to the four corners of the earth, or modern equivalent. He continued to hold the floor. Mesmerically.

'Now, you're all going to be given a task,' he barked, 'to sell crap to people who can't afford it and don't need it anyway.' His eyes bored through me as he held up what seemed to be an empty bottle. 'Fresh air,' he rasped in that rough-hewn hundred-a-day-man voice. 'Refills? Half price.' He slapped the bottle on the table. 'You've got till midnight, so why the hell are you still here?'

Two hours later I was stranded on Sink Estate of the Year with a van load of trainee sharks – Darrens, Sharons – and as I stood transfixed by the squalid scene before me, they knocked on door after door with wild-eyed, missionary zeal. Surrounded by burnt-out cars and boarded windows, broken glass and used syringes, I clutched my principles like a comfort blanket, with a suitcase full of empty bottles, my very own camera crew, and a rasping, barking, father-figure voice in my head: 'Do it!'

Timidly, I opened the suitcase and peered in. *Fresh Air*, it said. *Bottled At Source.* £6.99 seemed rather a lot for what, to these people, would be an unnecessary luxury, and yet my need for paternal approval overrode everything. I steeled myself to the task ahead and knocked on the first door. It was opened by a large man with a shaved head, hirsute shoulders, string vest.

'I wonder,' I said, 'if I could interest you in a bottle of fresh air.'

He slammed the door in my face. Good start. I had escaped with my life. Heart pounding, I scurried along the street. I was on a roll. Not that I'd actually sold any yet, but I was becoming battle-hardened. All I needed was the initial breakthrough. I rapped on a particularly sad-looking door. Paint peeling. Rusty handle. Cracked glass. No answer. I was about to try again when an ancient woman hobbled past.

'I think they're dead, son,' she croaked. She continued hobbling, stopped at the next door, fumbled for a key. I saw my opening.

'Let the dead bury their dead,' I quipped. 'But perhaps I could interest you in our latest product.' I whipped a bottle out and held it in front of her wizened old face as the camera crew moved in for a close up. 'Fresh Air.' She gave me a rheumy-eyed, quizzical look. I smiled enigmatically. 'Chateau Ballybough.'

I had chosen, at random, a well-known Dublin beauty spot. Good guess. Her face softened. 'Really, son?' she said. 'We used to take the tram out there every Sunday. Mind you, that was a long time ago.' She peered nostalgically at the bottle. 'Hold on, son. I have some money tucked away in case I wanted to eat this week.'

The door creaked open and she hobbled inside. I could hear her wheezing down the damp hallway and reflected that I had placed her accent well. I followed her in and watched as this tiny woman – as tiny in her own way as my mother had been in hers – lifted a small, dusty bowl from her damp mantelpiece and fingered her last sad coins into my blushing fist. She gripped the empty bottle with the full force of her nostalgia.

'God bless you son,' she said. 'I'll never forget your kindness to a poor old pauper woman a long way from home.'

I pointed out that poor and pauper were pretty much covering the same linguistic terrain, convinced her that a six pack formed the backbone of the modern shopping list, and let myself, and the camera crew, out.

Some time later I was back at Television House, facing a smouldering Sir Roger. He rasped at a couple of Sharons, then trained the finger of scorn on a Darren.

'What have you got to say for yourself, milksop?' he barked. Darren had nothing to say for himself. 'Spoken like a true wimp,' barked Sir Roger. 'Because that's what you are, milksop. A wimp! How many bottles have you sold? None, zero, zilch, you – *milquetoast*.' There was an air of suppressed violence in the room, and maybe Patriarchal Man sparked something off, or maybe it was the poor old pauper in her dark, damp flat, but my blood was up. I clenched my fists and festered. 'That goes for the lot of you,' barked Sir Roger. 'I was supposed to weed you out one by one. Week by week. But you're all weeds. All of you. One exception. This,' he rasped, jabbing his finger in my direction, 'is the man. You're all fired. He's hired. End of story. So what do you say to *that*?'

They had nothing to say to that. I, on the other hand, was seething. Maybe I should have stood up to my overbearing father all those years ago. The bullying. The abuse. The improper use of a mangle. As soon as Sir Roger had finished barking, rasping and jabbing, I was on my feet.

'I have this to say,' I exploded, jabbing a finger back at his jabbing finger. 'You're a bully. I don't like you and I don't like your ways.' I went on to launch a blistering attack on his creed of profit before people; of sell anything, but sell; of destroy our children's birthright, and our children's children's, before raising my voice for the final onslaught. 'Thanks to your creed of greed, a dear, sweet, consumptive old orphan woman will starve to death next door to her next-door neighbours who are also, apparently, dead.' Not a very well structured sentence, granted, but I was angry, and the words tumbled out as they saw fit.

Silence. Sir Roger sat rigid in his seat. The tension was palpable. And then?

'I'm terribly sorry,' he rasped gently. 'I've got something in my eye.'

He stood up and walked slowly out of the room, dabbing his eyes with a tissue supplied by a startled flunky. As soon as he was gone a Darren turned to me.

'Congratulations, mate,' he sneered. 'You've just talked yourself out of a hundred grand with your fluffy bunny crap.'

A hundred grand?! Why, that would more than pay off the mortgage arrears. I quickly wound back my anti-capitalist rant for possible loopholes. There weren't any. It postulated a world-view that made perfect sense. But – and it was a reassuring but – there was nothing in it that couldn't be clarified by saying the exact opposite; and so, as a dry-eyed Sir Roger returned to the room, my mind was made up. I had decided to reposition my moral compass.

'If I could just clarify a couple of points,' I began, but

my erstwhile father figure raised a hand for silence.

'Your words have touched me,' he trembled. 'Touched me to the deep heart's core. When I was outside just now I had time to reflect. That poor woman, I thought, could have been my dear old mum.' He sighed tragically. 'I've just seen the camera footage. She *is* my dear old mum. Parted at birth, but I never forget a face.' He wrestled with his inner demons and finally braced himself. 'It's never too late to change. I propose, as from today, to devote the rest of my life to being a truly good person. To donate my vast wealth to charity.'

And with that he wiped away a tear of gratitude and left the room. The stunned silence which followed was broken only by another stunned silence. A hundred grand? I couldn't just leave it there. I leapt to my feet and made for the door. I raced along the labyrinthine corridors of Television House. No sign of Sir Roger. I rushed outside. A stretch Rolls parked at the exit suggested there was still hope. I charged over. The chauffeur sat slumped dejectedly over the steering wheel. A large *For Sale* sign was plastered to the windscreen, and, off in the distance, a reborn Sir Roger hopped lightly aboard a double-decker bus.

I swore inwardly, tossed my moral compass at a nearby bin[12], and headed, with a heavy heart, for home. Blaise sat, also with a heavy heart, at the kitchen table.

Deceased mother? Lack of chocolate in the bloodstream?

'I thought I asked you to deliver my poem,' she said in her small, hurt voice. Enough to break your heart, frankly, if you happened to be looking in her direction at

---

[12] It fell to the ground, but what the hell. Aren't people paid to clean up?

the same time. I averted my gaze.

'I did,' I said.

'So what's this?' she asked, flicking a sheet of paper across the table. I gave it the once over. Words like *dappled, azure, opalescent* and *shards* swam before my eyes. Yup. That was a poem all right. I was about to argue that she shouldn't have left two poems lying about when she informed me, still with the slight edge of hurt, that she was off to the shops. If, that was, she could locate the shopping list.

I kept my own counsel on that one, but resolved to brush up on my modern poetry to avoid a repetition. Blaise, for her part, wrote a replica shopping list and remained quiet for the rest of the week. No answering the phone. No reading her mail. No leaping naked through the bracken. Just a stoic and resigned wait for the bailiffs.

By Friday morning I could stand it no longer. I decided to have a last listen to the radio before the bailiffs arrived to remove it.

'The poet, who was unavailable for comment,' it said, 'won with a savage indictment of domestic so-called bliss. The judges were unanimous. Her use of a shopping list to suggest domestic stasis was both hysterically funny and chillingly apposite. Read it, but be warned. You'll never eat broccoli again.'

I glanced at her replica list for hidden meanings. Curious. She'd written a whole new poem.

> *Peppermint crisps*
> *Walnut whips*
> *As many boxes of chocolate as can be fitted*
> *into the back of the car*
> *with the seat removed*
> *Rolos*

It went on for several pages and possibly required pruning, but I was beginning to get the hang of blank verse; and this poem, which was much more celebratory in tone than her previous offering, would be perfect for next year's competition.

I switched the radio off and went in search of Blaise.

Little did she know it, but things were about to get a whole lot better.

Occasions of Sin

I'd just been leafing through the Glasgow Film Theatre programme. *Occasions of Sin*. One night only. We simply had to go.

'Guess what?' I said, waving the programme excitedly like the schoolboy I'd been when the documentary was made. Blaise peered round the bathroom door, face half on.

'What?'

'*Occasions of Sin*,' I said. 'It's on at the GFT. One night only. We simply have to go.'

'Nice title,' said Blaise. 'What's it about?'

'Dublin,' I said. 'Early sixties. It was banned for, oh, *years*. This was Ireland, remember? The dark ages. It had things to say.'

'I'll bet it did,' said Blaise. 'Should be fascinating from a feminist perspective, too. You know. *Women: Role of*.'

'We didn't have women in those days,' I said. 'Mothers, yes. Nuns. I don't think women qua *women* came on the scene till I was well into my thirties.' I was in playful mood. Blaise narrowed her eyes. Possibly also playfully, difficult to tell.

'I need to see this,' she said. 'Call it research. So when's it on?'

'Tonight.'

'Ah.'

'Ah?'

'I've been asked to chair an event at the book festival.

One night only.'

'Tonight?'

'Tonight.'

'Ah.'

'Tell you what,' she said. 'Why don't you phone Dan? He's Irish. You can wallow in nostalgia together.'

Good idea, I thought. So I did. 'How's things?' I said.

'Fine,' he said. 'How's *your* things?' I said my things were fine. 'So,' said Dan. 'What's up?'

'*Occasions of Sin,*' I said. 'It's on at the GFT.'

I could feel Dan rubbing his hands together with erotic anticipation. 'Count me in.'

'Wrong genre, Dan,' I said. 'It's a documentary. Catholic church. Repressive state. Dickie Rock as Sex God. It might help explain how we turned out like we did.'

Dan looked confused at the other end of the line. 'So how *did* we turn out?' he said.

'Like this,' I said.

'Oh, right,' said Dan, and we left it at that.

The cinema was packed.

'You know what they say,' said Dan, as we made our way to our seats. 'Repressed sexuality sells.'

Good point. There were a lot of ageing hormones in there. Many of them Irish. We sat back as the lights went down. The thrill of it. Three seconds into the grainy footage of a bygone age Dan prodded me on the arm.

'Brings you back,' he whispered. I nodded politely. That was the whole point.

He prodded me every couple of minutes after that. Wasn't that O'Connell Street? Stephen's Green? Marino?

Prod prod prod. The camera then panned to a local school. Circa early sixties. I recognised it immediately and poked Dan on the shoulder.

'My old alma mater,' I whispered excitedly.

The camera passed through the big iron gate, across the schoolyard and in the main entrance; a journey I'd travelled many times in my youth. It was almost as if I *was* that camera. Nostalgia enveloped me like a huge pink blancmange. I may have sighed with happiness. I clasped Dan's little hand in mine. It should have been Blaise's little hand. It wasn't. Come to think of it, it wasn't even little. It was certainly bigger than I'd been expecting. Hairier. More gnarled. I whipped my own hand away and was about to explain the mix-up when, up on the screen, a classroom door opened, the camera went in and panned to a row of boys. Slightly unwashed by modern standards of hygiene. Ties askew. Thing is, I recognised them all at once[13]. It was my classroom! I was riveted. Strange. How had I forgotten the TV cameras coming to my school? I searched my memory – nothing. Yet there I was, about twelve years old, front row, sitting beside Henry McAdoo. Ye Gods! I recognised myself at once – I never forget a haircut.

Suddenly, the camera cut to our old Religious Knowledge teacher, Brother Boyle. The sight of his Brylcreem-flattened hair and flowing soutane raised nostalgia to a whole new level. Beside him stood a corpulent bishop in full episcopal regalia. 'Festering', as Brother Boyle was affectionately known, rubbed his

---

[13] Des Connell and Archie McQuaid. Larry O'Toole and Mick Boyle. Artie Smyth and Bobby Fowler. Don Caird and Edmund Byrne. Kevin McNamara and Diarmuid Martin. Fulk Bassett. I name them for the magic of it.

hands together unctuously. *'Any questions for the bishop, bize?'* he said.

The camera panned to the class. Thirty six hands shot up. This had an orchestrated look to it, probably because it was orchestrated. Brother Boyle pointed to Dermot Ryan. Dermot preened himself and looked self-important. His question: *'What's an occasion of sin, your worship?'*

Obviously a plant. You don't just think up stuff like that. Festering beamed approval. The bishop rippled with suppressed mirth. *'Well now,'* he said. *'You have me impaled on the horns of an exquisite dilemma there. An occasion of sin, my child, would be anything that leads a hot-blooded male boy from the path of righteousness. A lady of the female persuasion, now, would be top of my particular list.'* He turned to Brother Boyle with a knowing wink. *'I hope I'm allowed to say that, Brother,'* he rippled.

'Oh, now,' simpered an uncharacteristically servile Brother Boyle. *'Ladies is it, the Lord save us? Oh, now. Any other questions, bize?'*

The camera panned back to the class. Two hands shot up. Dermot Ryan's, naturally. Mine.

Mine?!

'That boy there,' said the bishop. *'Dermot,'* simpered Festering. *'No no,'* said the bishop. *'The one with the big eyes and the pink gansey.'*

I sat bolt upright in the cinema seat and almost held Dan's hand again, knowing whose hand it was this time. The camera panned back to my younger self: my period haircut, my pink gansey, my big, innocent eyes. My younger self spoke. *'Would your mammy be an occasion of sin, Father?'*

Time stood still for an everlasting moment. The unearthly silence before an explosion. Moment over, the cinema audience erupted with unrestrained hilarity. The camera swung back to the bishop. *'It's not Father, my child. I'm a bishop.'* 'Sorry, Father,' I said. *'But would she?'*

The bishop moved forward, raised a horny Catholic hand, and rearranged his eyes into mean little slits. *'Well if she is, my child, I'd keep it to yourself.'*

The hand whipped across my face. CRACK!

I froze in horror as this long-suppressed memory resurfaced. The humiliation. The jeering after school. The mother jokes. The film then cut to a beautiful shot of Dublin bay by night.

Dan nudged me. 'Would your mammy be an occasion of sin, Father?' he mimicked, then leaned over and lowered his voice for comic effect. 'Mine wouldn't anyway. Not with that moustache.'

Blaise was in when I got home. 'Well?' she said. 'Did it take you back?'

'It was very – educational,' I said. I may have been a bit downbeat, because Blaise got all – the only word I can think of is *maternal*.

'Aw, look at his little face,' she said. 'Come to – '

'Stop it right there,' I said. 'Please.'

Blaise looked upset. 'Look, I'm really sorry I couldn't make it,' she said. 'Still, I'd bet *anything* they'll put it out on DVD. Then we can watch it together. '

I froze inwardly. 'You think so?'

'I'd put money on it,' said Blaise. 'There must be a huge market out there. *I'd* buy it and I'm not even *Irish*.'

She came over and put her arms round me. 'Sorry I couldn't go. Still, maybe I can make it up to you in other ways. Bedroom's that way.'

Interesting twist. Perhaps Blaise had mistaken my hurt, possibly even sulky look, for moody and magnificent. I decided to dispense with my nightly cup of hot chocolate and see what fate had in store.

'I'll be through in a minute,' said Blaise. 'Something I have to do first.' I lay in bed wondering what that something might be. I distinctly heard the erotic rustle of silk emanating from the living room; I also inhaled an equally distinct whiff of *mystique* floating in from the bathroom; and was that not the click-click-click of stilettos on the lino?

Funny how the mind plays tricks. Blaise came in five minutes later fully dressed. Jeans. Cardy. Slippers – no heels. Exactly what she'd been wearing when we'd last spoken. I cooled down to room temperature instantly. Blaise disrobed in seconds and slipped in beside me.

'Guess what *I've* been up to,' she said. She had her seductive voice on. I was momentarily thrown. Had I imagined the jeans, the jacket, the absence of heels? No. She was dressed functionally for bed. What I call her good-night's-sleep-outfit. She moved closer. 'I've just been on the Internet and you're not going to believe this, but – it's already out on DVD!!!' My heart sank. 'So I clicked next day delivery. We *will* get to watch it together. Happy?'

In a word? No. In fact, happy was exactly what I *wasn't*. 'That's – that's great,' I said, and, although I normally steer well clear of the word, 'Triff.'

Sadly, her attempts at seduction came to naught as

I rolled up into a ball and metaphorically sucked my thumb.

'Poor boy,' she said. 'Poor, poor boy. We'll watch it together next time. Promise.'

She began stroking my back in a soft and loving way, but all I could think of as I drifted into sleep was the derisive laughter of the audience and Dan's gnarled hand.

I intercepted the DVD. I'm not proud of it, but what was I to do? I'd suffered enough. In the penal system of the Catholic afterlife it was a venial, not a mortal sin. A few thousand years of purgatory seemed a small price to pay for depositing the offending article in a nearby skip. Blaise was very busy over the next few days, so no harm done. She seemed, mercifully, to have forgotten all about it.

We were strolling down Byres Road later in the week. Unencumbered by the weight of my own past I felt positively – what's the word I'm looking for? – jocund. Blaise's soft hand in mine. The sky a delirious shade of what can only be described as blue. We were about to pop into the latest in a growing chain of pop-up shops when out popped Dan.

'So,' he said. 'How's things?' I was about to say that things were fine and ask him how his things were when he held a small bag up. 'You'll never guess what *I* got.'

Under the stone face and deeply unhappy moustache his eyes danced with mischief and glee.

'It's a bag,' said Blaise.

'Ah yes,' he said. 'It's a bag all right, it would be rather foolish to deny it. But what, pray, are the secrets that lie therein?'

He didn't wait for an answer. No. Like the simpleton he so obviously was he whipped out a copy of *Occasions of Sin*. I stared at him in disbelief. He mistook it, the fool, for delight.

'99p,' he said. 'Cash.'

'That's great, Dan,' said Blaise. 'We ordered one online but it never arrived. Tell you what, you two boys discuss your things, I'll pop in and get a copy for us.'

Dan held the DVD up. 'Last one, I'm afraid.' His eyes twinkled and he looked infuriatingly pleased with himself. I should have spotted the warning signs, but I didn't. He whipped another DVD out of the bag. 'Second last copy,' he said, thrusting the accursed thing at me. 'Go on. You know you want it.'

The imbecile preened himself as he refused payment. I may have looked less than ecstatic. Difficult to tell. Blaise nudged me impishly.

'Well?' she said. 'Aren't you going to say thank you to the nice man?'

That evening I tried to get Blaise to watch a documentary on *The Development of Theoretical Feminism in the Dutch East Indies 1412-17*, but as she pointed out, we'd watched it three times already and I'd fallen asleep, left the room and attempted suicide, though not necessarily in that order. So Blaise inserted *Occasions of Sin* into the machine. She also took control of the controls, slipped her arm through mine and clicked go. *O'Connell Street. Stephen's Green. Marino.* I was condemned to relive the long-suppressed memory of this deep, deep trauma again.

The camera rested on the wrought iron gates of my old school. It went in. I tried to censor it mentally. No use. *It moved inexorably on. Across the hall. Into the classroom.* Blaise's hold tightened. *The camera rested on the corpulent bishop.*

'My God,' breathed Blaise. 'The horror. The horror.'

I sat transfixed as the scene played out. Exactly as before.

Festering rubbed his hands together unctuously. 'Any questions for the bishop, bize?' Brother Boyle pointed to Dermot Ryan. Still preening himself, still looking self-important. 'What's an occasion of sin, your worship?'

Blaise smiled expectantly.

Festering beamed approval. The bishop rippled with suppressed mirth. 'Well, now. You have me impaled on the horns of an exquisite dilemma there. A lady of the female persuasion would be top of my particular list.'

Blaise erupted in a fit of giggles. 'Thought so.'

'Any other questions, bize?'

'That boy there,' said the bishop. *'The one with the big eyes and the pink gansey.'* I steeled myself. *The camera zoomed in on me; wide-eyed, pink-ganzied, about to humiliate myself.* Blaise lifted the control and clicked pause. The past stood still. She moved closer.

'What a gorgeous wee boy,' she said, and clicked continue.

'Would your mammy be an occasion of sin, Father?'

I awaited the hoot of derision.

Blaise sighed. 'I wish I'd known *you* when you were ten,' she said.

I bridled. 'Twelve,' I said. 'I was – ' Whoops.

The camera swung back to the bishop.

'It's not Father, my child. I'm a bishop.'
'Sorry, Father. But would she?'
The bishop moved towards me. He raised a horny Catholic hand, and rearranged his eyes into mean little slits.

Blaise slipped her hand into mine and spoke over the bishop. 'Bit of a rebel,' she said. 'My kind of – '

CRACK!

Blaise's hand tightened on mine.

A small hand.

An angry hand.

The hand of unconditional love.

The camera cut to a shot of Dublin Bay by night.

We fell silent. I relaxed. The danger was past. I closed my eyes in silent thanks. Man of a certain age. Watching a DVD about his native home in the year of Our Lord 1961 with his very own occasion of sin.

And this time she was dressed for it.

You Have The Right To Remain Silent

Picture the scene. A young man sits on a bridge over the Clyde, dangling his feet and staring out at the river. Lost in thought. Smoking. I'm strolling across the bridge. It's a bright, sunny day. I'm in fun-loving mood.

'Don't do it, young man,' I shout skittishly. 'You have your whole life ahead of you.' The young man turns, I smack into a lamppost, the young man laughs. A bit callous under the circumstances? I stagger about in pain, hand clamped over my blood-gushing nose, and walk unsteadily on. The young man's laughter follows me across the bridge. Cut.

When I arrived home – reeling slightly but otherwise compos mentis – Blaise was in her study. Her please-do-not-disturb sign had been amended. *Please* had been removed. *Do Not Disturb* had been enlarged. Several exclamation marks had been added[14]. The witty footnote[15] now had its own footnote, in which I was given a namecheck. She'd even given my date of birth and present address to avoid, as she explained in a further footnote, any confusion as to who exactly she had in mind. A tad harsh, perhaps, but a quadruple footnote brooks no argument, so I took my still-throbbing and bloodied nose into the bathroom. I would minister to my own needs, being by nature a stoic, and not given

---

[14] !!!
[15] The *That means you* one.

to whingeing simply because my features have been mangled beyond repair. Blaise, when she'd finished writing, would follow the trail of blood and weep.

Moments later, however, I managed to upset the bathroom cabinet, purely accidentally – I couldn't see a bloody thing – and the clatter as it crashed earthwards brought Blaise rushing from her study.

'What have you done to your poor *nose?*' she gasped, negotiating the contents of the cabinet as she raced towards me in a state of transparent shock.

I tried to explain that I had done nothing to my poor nose. That whatever had been done had been done by a lamppost. Blaise said nothing. She sat me down, dabbed my face with one of her many unguents, and suggested I avoid rogue lampposts, at least during the recovery period. This may have been a joke. Difficult to tell, as there was something almost maternal in her tone which suggested that she too blamed the post.

I avoided the great outdoors as a precautionary measure, and a few days later the incident had been filed away, as the nose healed itself and the great river of life flowed inexorably on. We'd finished breakfast and were listening to the news. The usual litany of disaster. I was just wishing there was something we could *do* when they cut to the obligatory good news story. From Glasgow, no less. A young man had been saved from suicide a few days earlier. His life had been an unending catalogue of missed opportunities and self-inflicted misery – no excuses. He'd opted for the finality of the Big S. Seems he'd been sitting on a bridge over the Clyde, smoking a last e-cigarette when a passing stranger – long black coat, grey hair, Irish accent – made him rethink his decision to end it all. How had he done this? Through the healing power of laughter.

The would-be suicide was now sobbing openly. He wanted to meet this man. He wanted to hug him. To thank him. He wanted to show the world there was still some goodness left in this vale of tears we call life. I may have embellished a bit here, but his wonderfully moving little paean to this remarkable individual ended with a plea to the man in question.

Come forward.

Please.

Make yourself known.

I want to thank you for saving my life.

Where there was darkness now there is light.

Where there was despair now there is hope.

Where there was –

'Oh, for fuck's sake,' said Blaise, hitting the 'off' button.

Eh?!

'Well,' she said, 'why does everything have to be so public? So someone saved his life. Let the poor sod be. Next thing you know he'll have an exclusive deal with the *Daily Mail* and everyone will hate him. I mean, whatever happened to unassuming modesty?' Enough with the speechifying, I thought, but she wasn't finished yet. 'When I was a wee girl,' she continued, going all Scottish on me as she's inclined to do whenever she gets emotional, 'if someone saved your life you thanked them privately. *Say thank you to the nice lady for saving your life. That's quite all right. You're welcome. Bye now.* These days the whole world has to know. It's so – *tacky.*'

Blaise's cheeks had rouged slightly. They always do when she's animated. I sat back down. Chastened.

'You're absolutely right,' I said. 'But you never know. He might not come forward. Might be one of those strong, silent types. Old school.'

'Hah,' said Blaise. 'Fat chance.'

'I wouldn't be so sure,' I said. 'Sounds like an excellent role model for the young. How was he described again? An inspirational slightly older man.'

'They didn't say slightly,' said Blaise. 'Just older.' A detail. I decided to let it pass. 'Come to think of it,' Blaise giggled, 'they didn't say inspirational either.'

'Maybe not,' I said, 'but my bet is he'll lie low till the fuss dies down and just take a quiet pleasure in knowing he's made the world a slightly better place.' I could tell by the way Blaise looked at me that she wasn't so sure. 'Maybe it's a man thing,' I said. 'The strong, silent type. You know. First chap up Everest in a pair of brogues. Kept it to himself. Well, *I've* never heard of him.'

Now I haven't read the Bible myself – it wasn't that sort of childhood – but I developed a passing interest, over the following days, in the story of the Good Samaritan. Here was a man who helped another man on the road to Jericho. I say road. Probably a dirt track. Yet two thousand years later, this *'small act of kindness'* (sic) is featured prominently in the best-selling publication the world has ever known. So how did *that* happen? I was mulling this over when Blaise interrupted.

'What's up with *you*?' she asked.

'Me?' I said. 'Nothing.'

'So why the smug look?'

'I was thinking about the Bible,' I replied.

'Ah,' said Blaise. 'That explains it.'

No, I thought. It doesn't. But I didn't say that. No point.

'You know the Good Samaritan,' I said.

'Wonderful woman,' said Blaise. 'What about her?'

I decided to start at the beginning. 'Well for a start she's a he.'

'You and your theories,' said Blaise. 'But do go on.'

'Okay,' I said, 'so let's have it your way. This Good Samaritan is wandering along minding her own business, thinking about the patriarchy and how much better things would be if the Middle East was run by women – '

'You've certainly done your research,' said Blaise.

'She sees this poor sod lying by the side of the road, doesn't pass by, and twenty minutes later she's kick-started the caring professions. So how do you think she got found out?'

'Sorry,' said Blaise, 'I don't follow.'

'Well, she could have just walked on with – what was it again? Unassuming modesty. End of story. So how did we get to hear of this iconic act of altruism?'

Blaise may have sensed a trap being set. 'Word of mouth, I suppose.'

'Fair enough,' I said. 'But whose mouth? There were only two of them there.'

Blaise shrugged. 'Well then, I suppose, take your pick.'

'Exactly what I've done,' I exulted. 'Now bear in mind that the story is leaked to the Bible. Would you want to go down in history as the man lying at the side of the road?'

Blaise shrugged again. She could see where this was going. 'Put like that,' she said, 'you probably have a point.'

'If, however, you've just dispensed a bit of totally selfless largesse,' I continued, 'you might be more inclined to pass it on.'

'Put like that,' said Blaise, 'ditto. Your overall point?'

'No point,' I said. 'Just curious.' I paused for effect. 'Thing is, though, it seems to me the Good Samaritan might just turn out to be a monstrous egotist. Note, for instance, the capital G in Good. Touch of self-mythologising going on there if you ask *me*.'

'Put like that,' said Blaise, 'I'm inclined to agree with you. In which case, she was probably a man after all.'

The media search for the unknown hero was on, but unsurprisingly – to me at any rate – no-one came forward. I checked the news bulletins for several days but, mindful of Blaise's views on the matter, I refrained from solving the mystery.

The following Saturday afternoon. Blaise and I were out for a leisurely stroll along Byres Road. A perambulation if you like. It's that sort of area. Lovely part of town. Cafés, students, arty types. I normally wander along in vacant or possibly pensive mood, the sound of Blaise's voice like the song of the blackbird, or the piccolo bit at the end of that symphony by what's-his-name. Background, but beautiful with it.

On this occasion, however, I was in a state of heightened awareness.

'Mind the glass door, madam. Potentially lethal.' 'Careful

of the kerb there, lad. Deceptive drop.' That sort of thing.

'Are you okay?' asked Blaise.

'Just doing my bit,' I said, as I helped an old man locate the hole in the post box. 'Let's just say I found a certain person pretty damned inspirational.'

'Really?' said Blaise. 'And who exactly would that be?' I gave her hand an affectionate squeeze and said nothing. We perambulated on.

Now I may have failed to mention my friend and compatriot Dan[16]. A Dubliner like myself, he has a long face, best described, perhaps, as lugubrious. With matching walrus moustache[17]. And here he was.

'Heard about the Secret Samaritan?' he said. No preamble.

'Vaguely,' I said, easing him away from the kerb – you can't be too careful these days. 'Just the bare bones. You know, nothing too detailed.'

'It was in the news again at lunchtime,' said Dan.

'Must've been a slow day,' said Blaise.

'That'll be it,' said Dan. '*Israel to relocate to New York State. City of London declared insolvent.* Apart from that – '

He may have laughed at his own joke. Difficult to say with that moustache. I decided to steer the conversation back to the subject matter.

'Inspirational figure,' I said. 'We must guard against cynicism.'

---

[16] Why *should* I mention him? This, after all, is a book about Blaise. I read a writing manual once and it said 'Keep your camera on the story.' I stopped reading at that point. The author was obviously delusional. You don't write with a camera. But on mature reflection, I realised, it did make an odd sort of sense. So. In *The Book of Blaise* I try to keep the camera on the subject matter. Sort of soft focus. But let's say Dan has just wandered into shot. The camera is now on him.

[17] Which also wandered into shot.

'Thing is,' said Dan, 'the Daily Mail has offered a reward.'

'Really?' I said.

I toyed with the idea of telling Blaise all. She could locate the man. He – in this case I – would own up to everything and take the consequences. We would be modestly wealthy. The world would be a better place. Everyone a winner.

'Did you know he's Irish?' asked Dan.

'Big deal,' said Blaise. 'So's half the population of America.'

'Two thirds,' said Dan. 'At least. We can probably rule the vast majority out, though. For a start, most of them would have been in America at the time. Or tracing their ancestry in West Cork.'

Good point. I was about to suggest that the bridge in question – not half a mile from where we stood – would be a detour too far, even from West Cork, but Blaise was off again. 'It's obscene,' she spluttered. 'You can't do a good deed, these days, without being dragged all over the media.'

Talk about changing the subject. Dan, after all, had begun the task of narrowing the search for this remarkable man. Irish. Slightly older. Probably lived locally. It was certainly something to be going on with.

'He's obviously gone to ground,' said Blaise. 'Good for him.'

'I doubt he'll stay anonymous long,' said Dan, leaning in conspiratorially. 'Seems they found some CCTV footage.'

'Really?' I said.

Dan took his mobile out, scrolled for a while, then

held it up for us to see. 'Bit grainy,' he said, 'or maybe that's just him.'

Blaise studied the image. I stayed aloof, merely glancing as it passed from Dan to Blaise. But yes, that was me all right, in my long black coat. It was one of those eureka moments where I could fully understand why Blaise found me so damned physically attractive.

'He reminds me of someone,' said Blaise, 'but I can't quite work out who.' I could have nudged her in the right direction, but let her work it out for herself, I thought. Instead of which, she decided to go off on one of her endearing little rants. 'I mean look at him,' she said. 'Late forties-ish?' Flattering, but I could take it. 'Looks like a man in a stable relationship. See? He doesn't dress himself, plus the haircut works. Mr. Bum-in-the-butter, *I'd* say.' Self-flattery did she but know it. I said nothing. 'Now let's imagine him in a year's time if his secret gets out. He's become unbearably smug. His loving partner has left him because if there's one thing she can't stand it's unbearably smug. No loving partner to look after him so he has to choose his own trousers.' I seem to recall a climax involving drugs, loose floozies and not phoning his mother, but I'd zoned out by that stage. To be honest, I was thinking how sexy I must look in that coat to a certain type of passerby[18].

'Well?' said Blaise. I noticed she was looking at me. One of her amused looks for some reason.

'Spot on,' I said. 'Couldn't agree more.'

While this little scene was unfolding a small group had formed. Some were taking photos. Others stared in our direction. I was, it seems, about to be unmasked. A

---

[18] m stroke f.

pretty shocking turn of events as I had done so much to hide my identity and protect my loved ones from the inevitable media storm. Ah well. *C'est,* as the French have it, *la vie. Whatever will be will be.*

I turned my best side to the mobiles and feigned nonchalance. 'So how are things, Dan?' I said.

'Ah, you know yourself,' he said. I didn't actually, so I said nothing. He would elaborate in his own good time. 'Lost the job,' he elaborated eventually. 'Still, you know what they say.'

I didn't actually, so I said nothing. Neither did he. Blaise, however, who wasn't au fait with the unwritten rules of male conversation, broke the silence.

'That's terrible, Dan,' she said.

'Ah, you know yourself,' said Dan stoically.

'No, Dan,' said Blaise. 'I don't.'

'It's the kids who suffer,' sighed Dan. 'Well, got to go.'

We watched him walk away, his back the back of a man broken on the grinding wheel of early twenty-first century Capitalism.

'Poor man,' said Blaise. 'How many children has he?'

'Two?' I said. 'Six?'

A quizzical look suggested that Blaise found this odd. 'You've known him for years,' she said. 'Surely you must have met his children at some point.'

Another case of Blaise's failure of the imagination vis-à-vis male inter-relationships. Children are off limits in casual conversation. Besides, other people's children are like kittens in a basket. They frolic about the place, which makes them impossible to count even if you were that way inclined. But I said nothing. I was preoccupied.

The small group of photographers had expanded, it was still frantically clicking away, and it was following my old friend Dan along the street, recording his every step. But – why? I was trying to process this unexpected turn of events when Blaise's friend Faye spotted us from the other side of the road and rushed across.

'Hi, guys,' she beamed. 'What's, like, happ'nin'?'

'Nothing much,' said Blaise. 'You?'

'I'm just off to see that Sylvia Plath tribute act in the library,' said Faye.

'Really?' said Blaise. 'How come no-one told *us*?'

I seemed to remember binning a couple of flyers but pretended to be deep in thought. Faye punched me playfully on the arm.

'You,' she teased. 'Anyway, you know now. Plus I've got an extra ticket.' she waved it gaily in the air. 'So who's the lucky lady?' She winked at me. 'Clue's in the gender.'

Blaise squeezed my hand. 'Not your thing,' she said. 'Besides, you look as though you could do with a nice long walk. Why don't you go for a ramble by the river?'

Funny, I thought, how Blaise understands these things at a deep level. I harboured a great secret and needed to be alone. At the same time, and I'm about to contradict myself here, I harboured a great secret – and had to tell *someone*. If it had been three in the morning, and I'd been drunk, and the barman had been polishing glasses, I probably would have confided in *him*. Possibly in black and white with a melancholy pianist tinkling in the background. But those days are gone. So where else *was* there? As I wandered away from Blaise and Fay, I gave myself over to the contemplation of that most profound of questions. Where else, I repeat, was there?

As I was trying to think of somewhere, anywhere, I passed a Catholic church. Divine intervention? Fate? It's not for me to say, but I hadn't been inside a church for many years and I wasn't about to waver in my unbelief now. So I walked on. But wait. Surely there was no harm in a bit of harmless banter with a priest? Nothing too heavy. No commitment either way.

So in I went. As soon as I walked out of the sunlight into the soothing shadow of the church I realised I'd done the right thing. I felt better already. As if a huge weight had been lifted from my shoulders. A heavy boulder, say, or one of Blaise's suitcases. The one with the broken handle.

I was about to sit in a pew and await further developments when I heard a muffled sobbing from the confessional. Fate again? Divine intervention twice in the same day? Not for me to say, but the anonymity of the confession box was exactly what I needed. No-one else was waiting, so I slipped into the empty cubicle and closed the door onto darkness. The sobbing continued. I continued to wait. Ten minutes later it struck me. There was no penitent in the other cubicle. It was the priest himself who was sobbing.

'Are you okay in there?' I asked.

He wasn't. I knew that. But he was a man. You have to give them an out.

The shutter opened slowly.

'Ah,' he sighed in his mellifluous West Cork lilt, 'it gets on top of you so it does. *Forgive me Father this, Forgive me Father that.* Day after day after day. And I wouldn't mind, but here am I, stuck in this godforsaken hole in perpetuity *when I didn't feckin' do it.*' His voice rose an octave. 'Do you know what it is, I should be a bleddy bishop by now. Did I say bishop? Hah. Cardinal! At least.' He blew his nose and stifled a second sob. 'Anyway,' he said, 'what have *you* been up to?'

'Ah, you know,' I said. 'Bit of this, bit of that.'

'Is that what you came in to tell me?'

I took a deep breath. I'd been desperate to tell someone for days, and what better place than here? Confidentiality guaranteed. 'The thing is,' I began, 'I don't know if you've heard about the Good Samaritan?'

'Just a bit,' he said. 'The Road to Damascus fella[19].'

'I mean the new one,' I said.

'Oh,' he said. 'Him. The River Clyde guy. What about him?'

I leaned closer to the wire mesh. 'It's not *him*,' I said. 'It's *me*. I've pledged to keep it a secret, even from my nearest and dearest. But I had to confide in *someone*.'

I could hear him sitting up. 'I *see*,' he said. 'Well that puts an entirely different complexion on things, my child.' He leaned closer. 'Confide in *me*.'

So I did. I unburdened myself of everything. My greed: I told him about the reward. My petty vanities: I told him about my almost overwhelming desire to boast about it. Then I said something which was news to me even as I said it. 'To be honest,' I said, 'I even harbour bitter thoughts about my best and dearest friend Dan.'

'Do you tell me so?' said the priest. 'And why would that be now?'

'For stealing my glory,' I said. 'Simple as that. Oh, I can't say I like myself for it, but there it is. Last time I saw him, he was swanning down Byres Road pursued

---

[19] Wrong road, but what can you do?

by an adoring mob, and all I could think was, That should be me!'

'Go on, my child,' said the priest.

'Sorry?'

'You were getting a bit het up about this Dan fella,' said the priest.

I decided to stop there. I'd probably said too much already. 'That's about it,' I said.

The priest leaned over the grill. 'In that case,' he whispered, 'keep it to yourself for the greater glory of God.'

'But I don't believe in God,' I said.

'In *that* case,' said the padre, 'know that on the day of judgment you will come into your just punishment not once, not twice, but three times thrice.'

'But as I've said I don't believe in God, it sort of follows that I don't believe in the afterlife either,' I protested.

'Well then,' he said, possibly a bit testily at this stage, 'offer it up for the souls of the faithful departed.'

I didn't bother pursuing the matter. This could have gone on for hours.

'Fair enough,' I said. 'The souls it is.'

The priest leaned back and sighed. 'I think an Our Father and three Hail Marys should just about cover it,' he said, and he started giving me absolution in a sibilant and slightly rushed stage whisper. I left him to it and returned to the empty pew. I made a decent fist of the penance and left the church a possibly holier man.

By the time I arrived home I was back to my usual sunny self. I was about to locate Blaise and check if *she* was back to her usual sunny self, post-Sylvia, when I heard her voice from the living room.

'That's great news, Dan,' she said. 'And just at the right time too, with all those mouths to feed. I'll let him know as soon as he comes in. Ah, here he – Dan?' She put the phone down. 'That was Dan,' she said.

'I gathered that,' I said. 'Just come into some money, has he?'

Blaise didn't pick up on the tone. '*Sort* of,' she replied. 'He's just got a job at a call centre, so he wanted to let us know. Oh, and three.'

'Three?'

'He's got *three* children,' she chirruped as I followed her into the kitchen. 'Anyway, can you believe it? He was harassed all the way down Byres Road. Apparently everyone thought he was the Secret Samaritan. Irish, black coat, grey hair.'

I may have arched an eyebrow. 'Well?' I said. 'Isn't he?'

'Course not,' said Blaise. 'He told them to take a closer look at the footage. Cherchez le moustache. There wasn't one. Couldn't possibly be Dan. He's had that moustache since he was ten. End of story.'

Two days later Blaise came out of her study waving her laptop excitedly.

'Here, quick.' she said. 'Take a look at this.' I sat beside her on the sofa.

Live news broadcast. A Catholic priest. Irish. Grey hair. Long black coat. Holding a magnified-for-the-cameras cheque from the *Daily Mail*, and standing with his arm round the young man from the bridge.

'This munificent reward may be *for* me,' he lilted,

'but the life-affirming little episode which engendered it is not *about* me. No, it's about all of us, for this story tells us something about our common humanity.' He stared straight through the screen, oozing humility. 'Go ye and do likewise,' he said. 'For we are all that Secret Samaritan.'

'The Lord,' said Blaise, 'certainly moves in mysterious ways.' She closed the laptop and put her hand in mine. 'My hero,' she said, kissing me on the cheek. 'And you're right. You *do* look sexy in that coat.'

Scrotum

I studied my email inbox with mounting disbelief. Seven new messages, all offering penile extensions. Every morning, at least half a dozen of the damn things popped in at regular intervals. I mean, do these people stay up all night? I thought of bringing the matter up with Blaise, but the penis word tends to bring out her skittish side and besides, I'd just had an interesting thought; a way to deal with this relentless touting for business.

I went to the out-of-office reply bit and typed as follows:

I'm afraid I'm not at my laptop at the moment, but if you've just left a message about the length of my penis, with particular reference to its shortcomings-no-pun-intended, please consider this: In order to achieve the suggested nine inches we're not talking extensions. Quite the opposite in fact. Please send quote for a three-inch snip.

There. That should do it. Away-message on.

The following morning I opened my laptop with a certain sense of satisfaction. But what was this? Only an email from Bonnie! My beloved[20] daughter. Who *never* emails her father. I may have gasped.

'What's up?' said Blaise.

'Not a thing,' I said, tapping the table nervously. Blaise plucked a blueberry from the top of her breakfast yogurt and popped it in her mouth.

[20] (but arguably estranged)

'Well that's all right, then,' she said.

'You know the away-message thing,' I said. 'Does that go to everyone?'

'That's the general idea,' said Blaise. 'Queen and commoner. Rich woman, poor woman. Wise woman, fool. Why? What have you done now?'

'Untold damage,' I said.

Blaise put her spoon down. 'Go on.'

I repeated my away message. In full.

'I see,' said Blaise. 'So who exactly, present company excluded, now knows you have a twelve-inch penis?'

I clicked on Bonnie's email and read it out loud. 'Hi Dad. I'm writing a sitcom with Zack Zackariah. You got it. *The* Zack Zackariah. Big break or what? Anyway, we're in town doing some research so I thought I'd pop in. xxx Bonnie'

Blaise put her bowl down. 'Tell you what,' she said. 'Get straight back with an upbeat email. *Hi, honey, I'm home. Can't wait to see you.* Subliminal subtext: DISREGARD AWAY MESSAGE. Block capitals. With any luck she won't read it.'

Blaise went into her study muttering something about wise woman, fool. I was left to agonise alone. What would such a message do to an innocent and impressionable young mind? Bonnie was only – well, I was led to believe she was seventeen, but still. She'd be scarred for life. Doomed to years of therapy with some deranged head doctor in charge of her disintegrating psyche. Blaise's best friend Faye, for instance. What an appalling vista.

I emailed Bonnie as instructed, and agonised the hours away. Innocence, doom, therapy, Faye. This circular and nightmarish train of thought was eventually interrupted just after lunch by the doorbell. Bonnie's arrival with *the* Zack Zackariah. Blaise saw to that bit. Ushered them in. Sat them down. Did the small talk thing. I braced myself and made an entrance from the kitchen. The pre-planned unplanned entrance. Bonnie and her young male companion stared at me from the sofa. I feigned breezy.

'So,' I said. 'You got my email.' No tears or hysterical accusations. It seemed I was in the clear. I relaxed inside. Crisis over. Zack stood up. A gangly young man with a flop of black hair over one eye, he coughed diffidently.

'This is Zack, Dad,' said Bonnie.

'Pleased to meet you,' grinned Zack. 'I brought you, um – ' He held out a DVD box set. I looked at the cover. *Zack Zackariah IS Scrotum*[21]. Scrotum? My precious daughter was involved with a character called Scrotum! I decided to stick with breezy.

'This – ,' I said hoarsely, 'this is quite something.'

'Thought you'd be impressed, Dad,' said Bonnie.

At this point Blaise came in and did the tea tray thing – tea, sandwiches and the like – which gave me time to regroup. I focused my attention on the box set and turned to the back.

CONTAINS CLASSIC EPISODE
WILL THEY WON'T THEY!!!

Scrotum meets older woman on chat site.
Sets up blind date – turns out it's his mother.
Soft lights.
Few drinks.
Why not?

---

[21] *Phwoar Productions*

'So, Dad?' Bonnie beamed at me.

'Very – ' I began.

'Cutting edge?' suggested Blaise.

Bonnie turned to Zack. 'Told you he'd love it.'

I grabbed a sandwich. We all grabbed sandwiches. Well, except for Blaise. Her mobile went. She glanced at the number, winced, and decided to take it in her study. I waited till she'd closed the door. 'Her mother,' I said. I knew this from the wince. 'She lives in Trossach, Zack. Setting for *The Embalmers*. Ever seen it?' He looked confused. 'TV series. Black and white. Bit before your time. Bit before my time come to think of it. In fact,' – I was slipping naturally into jovial father-in-law mode here – 'I think it may have come out before Alexander Graham Bell invented the telly.'

Alexander Graham Bell didn't invent the telly – I checked later – but Zack didn't contradict me. Good sign. Polite. I'd moved on from *The Embalmers* and had just switched to an amusing anecdote about scout leader Hector Baden Powell and one of his more dubious brisk hikes[22], when Blaise came back into the room, looking harassed.

'What is it this time?' I said.

'She's just got cable TV,' said Blaise.

'Catastrophe,' I said. 'She'll be awash in pornography.'

'That's not it,' said Blaise.

'Don't tell me,' I said. 'She didn't need the aerial any more so she decided to take it down herself, and she's stuck. Again.'

---

[22] *A Brisk Hike Up The Trossachs* (pps 123-135): This anecdote involved, as always, the prettier members of F-troop, and what Baden Powell euphemistically termed *'outdoor pursuits'*. Removed from 2nd edn. after legal action by parents. Obscenity laws cited.

'Got it in one,' said Blaise. 'She's on the roof.'

I let the image sink in. Ancient Presbyterian on roof with mobile phone.

'So why,' I asked, 'didn't she phone the emergency services?'

'You know what she's like,' said Blaise.

I did. Old school. Dunkirk spirit. Or was it Bannockburn?

Blaise steeled herself. 'I'll have to go over.' She was already pulling her coat on.

'There's no way you're going on that roof on your own,' I said, jumping up from the sofa. 'I'm coming too.'

Blaise usually tried to talk me out of trips to Trossach. Isobel and me? Let's just say there's a tension there, and it has its roots in the tragic history of these islands. But this was serious. Isobel was one feisty octogenarian, but as with all octogenarians she was also pretty old, and this was a two-storey house. Blaise went in search of her car keys. I was about to explain the situation to Bonnie and Zack, but Bonnie was busy typing onto a laptop while Zack looked over her shoulder. You had to admire their industry. I coughed politely to get their attention.

'It's Blaise's mother,' I said.

Bonnie looked up from her laptop. 'We know,' she said.

'She's stuck on the roof.'

'Got that too,' said Bonnie.

'Thing is,' I said, 'I'm afraid we've got to mount a rescue operation.'

'Epic,' said Zack. Difficult to know exactly what he meant by epic, but I took it to mean he was impressed.

Bonnie closed her laptop with a look of – what? –

daughterly pride? 'Can we come?' she asked.

I was delighted. This really was an unexpected bonus. 'Our car is your car,' I said. 'Why not?'

'Awesome,' said Zack.

I was grilling Zack on his knowledge of television history as we entered Trossach. He'd never even heard of *The Embalmers*, so I was filling him in on its gallery of lovable rural archetypes, and how fans came from every country in the known world to pay homage, when we got stuck behind a coach disgorging large numbers of white-haired men onto the town square.

'Aha!' I gushed, delighted. 'Embalmies!' How was that for serendipity?

I was in my element by this stage, and launched into a pretty accurate impersonation of Dr. Cruikshank, the local GP and bane of the embalmers' lives. Older readers may remember him as the welcome comic relief. He never thought his patients were lost causes, even when they were dead. He also had an excellent catchphrase, which I was about to deliver in my best Highland accent. But why waste this glorious catchphrase on a four-seater when the perfect audience stood a matter of feet from the car? 'Watch this, folks!' I said as I opened the door and leapt gleefully out.

'Please don't,' said Blaise in her smallest, pleadingest voice, and how I wish I'd listened to her. Unless it's to do with chocolate I should always listen to her. But I didn't. I bounded over to the white-haired men, huddled together in what I later understood to be collective trauma.

'Get behind that screen, laddie,' I boomed, 'and take aff yer troosers till we get a good luke at you.'

To my surprise, not to mention perturbation, they scurried, whimpering pitifully to a man, back on board the coach; leaving behind a furious-looking woman with a clipboard and a large name tag. Dr. Morag McSomething. The old men, she informed me icily, were former charges of notorious scoutmaster Hector Baden Powell. The prettier members of F troop, no less, on a therapeutic day out from 'the home'. My little interjection, as Dr. Morag called it, had set them back *years*.

The sky darkened in sympathy. Passersby scowled and tutted in my direction. I trudged back to the car, chastened. Bonnie and Zack were still glued to their laptop, tapping away. That's a relief, I thought, as I slipped back into my seat. Apart from traumatising a generation of pensioners and upsetting a no doubt leading member of the psychiatric profession, I felt, no harm done.

As the coach thundered off Blaise slid into first. 'A small but pertinent detail in case it ever happens again,' she said. 'They were all wearing identical shorts.' Good point, I thought, but I said nothing.

This too would pass.

There was no sign of Isobel when we arrived at her house in John Knox Crescent. Just a tall ladder, fully extended, leaning against the front wall. I tried shouting at the roof – no response. Blaise checked all the rooms inside, upstairs and down, then tried her mobile – no response either.

'Probably clinging on to the aerial,' I said. 'I'm going up.'

'Mega,' said Zack. I could see he was beginning to view me as a role model. A sort of modern-day action-man-stroke-father-figure. I felt proud and not a little humbled as I braced myself for ascent. I may have puffed myself up slightly. I also imagined myself with a pair of large blue underpants outside my trousers, but this was momentary and may have owed something to reading too many comics as a child.

'Here,' said Blaise. 'Take the mobile, just in case.'

I slipped it in my pocket, stood at the foot of the ladder and looked up. Clouds scudded past the roof at an alarming speed. Is it possible to suffer vertigo at ground level? I wasn't sure, but I certainly experienced a ringing in my ears, a blurring of vision, and a distinct swirling sensation as if I was being whirled like a Dervish and sucked into the menacing sky. Certain lines came to mind. *There is some corner of a Scottish roof that is forever Dublin.* That's the thing about great poetry. You don't think about it from one day to the next, but there it is when you need it.

I began the upward climb. Rung by tentative rung. As I reached the top of the ladder I craned my neck and surveyed the vast expanse of grey slates. Still no sign of Isobel. No sign of an aerial either. I was trying to puzzle this out when the mobile rang. I gripped the ladder with fist-numbing intensity and tugged the phone from my pocket. As I clicked answer, Isobel's resonant tones cut across my hello.

'Blaise! You'd better come quickly. There's a man on my roof.'

'I know,' I bellowed courteously. 'I *am* that man.'

Isobel sounded shocked and relieved. 'Is that you, Dr.

O'Shaughnessy?' she said. 'What on earth are you doing with my daughter's phone? And why in God's name are you on my – don't tell me. You're Irish. The builder's gene has finally got the upper hand.' I gripped the ladder tighter as Isobel wittered on. 'Well, I must say I admire your industry. Doctoring is a full-time job, but I suppose you'll be supplementing your income. To be honest, I'm surprised some lucky woman hasn't snapped you up.'

'But I *have* been snapped up,' I said.

'Well, never mind about that now,' said Isobel. 'Perhaps you'd be so good as to check the chimney while you're up there. I may have been a bit rough with the aerial. Don't know my own strength, frankly. I also located a loose slate. Right side. Three rows from the gutter. I'm sure you'll know what to do. Oh, and by the way, if you happen to see that daughter of mine, tell her I've bought scones.' She paused meaningfully. 'Mingus loves his scones.'

'Mingus?' I said, my knuckles whitening from the strain of holding on.

'Her husband,' said Isobel. 'They make such a lovely couple. Why, they do *everything* together.'

There was bravado in her voice, but did I detect a slight undercurrent of hesitancy too? Almost as if she knew that I wasn't Dr. O'Shaughnessy; that the lucky woman who'd snapped me up was, in fact, her aforementioned daughter; and that Mingus now ate his beloved scones elsewhere. I was contemplating all this when a sudden gust of wind caught the ladder. I glanced down in terror. The ground span. I held on with jellified fingers as I promised to search out a little something for Isobel's lumbago. I could see Zack and Bonnie spinning far below – still, by the looks of it, hard at work on their script – as I dialled 999.

I finally reached ground level. We won't dwell on the details further than to say that the emergency services had a three day waiting list, so I made my own way down, to the apparent delight of a sizeable crowd of onlookers. I believe a speeded-up version, with piano accompaniment, is currently available on the internet[23].

But I digress. Back on mother earth there was still no sign of Isobel, so while Blaise put the kettle on, and Bonnie and Zack settled on the sofa, I searched for her remote control. It is *imperative* that the elderly be protected from the more hardcore type of output now deemed acceptable on mainstream television. As the remote control wasn't anywhere obvious, I searched the house systematically. Blaise found me, twenty minutes later, riffling through Isobel's underwear drawer. I held up an item with clasps, buckles and metal attachments. Blaise grabbed it, folded it as far as you can fold such a thing and returned it to the drawer.

'What on *earth* are you doing?' she said.

'I'm looking for Isobel's remote,' I said.

Blaise turned me, manually, in the direction of the door.

'She keeps it in her gadget box in front of the telly. Downstairs. Now.'

Blaise was right. Isobel's gadget box was, indeed, right

---

[23] Three million, two hundred and thirty thousand, four hundred and thirty two hits as I write, apparently, which beats my previous record by twenty six.

in front of the telly. It was large, it was black, it even had GADGET BOX written on the lid in block capitals, so why hadn't I spotted it before? I believe it's a brain thing. I wasn't looking for a GADGET BOX, I was looking for a remote, so the box was somehow invisible while my cognitive brain concentrated on the mental image of the remote. Well, something to that effect. But there in front of the telly was the GADGET BOX marked GADGET BOX, and there, inside it, was the remote, not to mention a roll of gaffer tape – and still no sign of Isobel.

Which allowed me to tape the remote without interruption. Isobel would thank me for it if she knew what I was saving her from. Smut, filth and downright lewdity. I left her with the BBC channels. I like to think of the BBC as the Church of England at play. Wrong denomination for an unreconstructed Presbyterian, but it wouldn't do her any lasting damage.

She came in shortly after I'd put the gaffer tape away, a bag of scones in one hand, a parcel in the other. She handed the scones to Blaise and sank back, exhausted, into her electric chair. Bonnie and Zack closed the laptop, sat up and smiled politely.

'You young people amuse yourselves,' groaned Isobel. 'I'll just rest here a wee while. As for you, Dr. O'Shaughnessy, perhaps you'd be so good as to pop this old thing in the bin.' She took the taped-up remote from the gadget box and tossed it in my direction. She then tore the parcel open like an excited child, all signs of exhaustion gone. I watched in reluctant admiration as she removed a space age gadget, flicked the back open, inserted batteries with practised ease and pointed the thing at her screen. Click. Click. Click click click. The screen burst into life.

CHANNEL E114! IT'S TOXIC!!!

Isobel settled back and sighed happily. 'E double one four,' she said. 'My favourite!' She turned to Zack for the first time and winked. 'They've got *Scrotum* on a loop.' She giggled like a superannuated schoolgirl. '*Will They Won't They?* Naughty boy.' Then she yawned and settled in for a sleepover at her own house and an all-night toxic pig-out.

As we bounced along the narrow roads on the return journey, Blaise demolished a therapeutic Toblerone. In the back, Bonnie and Zack were once more hard at work on their script. Mostly laughing helplessly at a particularly funny bit. *Dysfunctional Dad. Emergency call. Trip to the country.* I'm paraphrasing.

'I don't know where you two get your ideas,' said Blaise, but I felt that I, at least, was beginning to get the hang of their working methods. I listened intently. *Boy scout scene as flashback*, said Zack. *Cut to roof*, said Bonnie.

'Hold on,' whispered Bonnie. 'Haven't we forgotten something?'

'What?' said Zack.

'The nine-inch penis. Where do we get that in?'

And before I could stop myself I twisted round in my seat and out it popped.

'Twelve-inch,' I corrected. 'And shouldn't that be the climax?'

Bonnie sat up rigid. '*Dad*. I cannot *believe* you just said that. I mean that is so – ' she stopped mid-sentence, her face full of unaffected disgust.

'Actually,' said Zack, tapping furiously, 'he's right. That's *funny*.'

'Awesome!' said Bonnie, and all I could hear, for some time afterwards, was the sound of frantic tap-tapping.

Blaise squeezed my hand reassuringly.

We drove on.

Fade to credits.

The C Word

I sat on the bed as Blaise pulled dress after dress from the wardrobe and tossed them over a chair already piled high with dresses.

'Nothing fits!' she wailed.

Of course they didn't fit, and I could have quite easily explained why. She always insists on buying dresses two sizes too small. I thought of pointing this out, but decided against as a mauve wool tunic flew past my left ear.

The chair full, she started using the bed. I moved discreetly to one side.

'Thing is,' she continued to wail, 'I'm introducing Treasure Mbotze at the Women's Library in four weeks' – she tossed a fetching blue chemise onto the ever-growing pile – 'and I have nothing to wear. I mean have you *seen* Treasure Mbotze? She's *stunning*.'

'Who?' I said.

'We've been through all this,' sighed Blaise. 'Treasure Mbotze? The celebrated novelist? International Women's Day?'

'Ah,' I said. '*That* Treasure Mbotze.'

'And nothing fits!'

'Well, buy something,' I said.

'I've just bought *this*!' Blaise tossed a silky black dress in my direction.

'So what's the problem?' I said.

'It's two sizes too small.'

She sat on the end of the bed. The weight proved too

much. The bed crashed through the floorboards into the basement and we were both killed instantaneously. Actually, that was me being intentionally humorous. Blaise sat on the bed and I put a comforting arm around her shoulder.

'Well, buy something else,' I said.

So she did.

As Blaise held up yet another dress in the reduced section a dainty assistant, all manicured nails and blonde hair, materialised at her elbow.

'If madame requires any help – ' she began.

'Actually,' said Blaise, peering closely at the dress, 'there's a split in the lining.'

'Ah, yes,' sighed the assistant. 'Bit of a history, that. A lady decided to try it on a few days ago. I advised discreetly against, of course, but she just wouldn't listen. Forced herself into it. *Far* too small. Then you'll *never* guess what – ' She paused.

'What?' said Blaise.

The assistant lowered her voice. Conspiratorially.

'Couldn't get it off, could she? Too embarrassed to come back out. Got stuck in the back window. Had to be winched out. As I said to the fire officer at the time, eighteen into twelve simply will not go.'

'I'll try it on,' said Blaise.

The assistant looked Blaise up and down and coughed politely. 'Is madame quite sure?'

Blaise bridled discreetly, took the dress and disappeared through a door marked fitting rooms. Madame *was* quite sure. I was left, yet again, to my own devices. It brought me back to a similar scenario with my beloved daughter, Bonnie, many years previously. Different shop. Kiddies' section. Bonnie was trying a couple of dozen items on in the changing room. I was passing the time fingering the merchandise, and marvelling at the prices, when I spotted an assistant giving me sideways glances. Always a bad sign. I decided to put her at her ease. 'Is it just me,' I said, 'or is it hot in here?' Odd how the most innocent of remarks can be wilfully misinterpreted.

I was thinking about the fallout when I was eased back to the present by a buzzing sensation in my left trouser pocket. A not displeasing sensation I'd have to say, which is why it took some time to filter through. Turns out it was my mobile, which stopped buzzing as soon as I grabbed it.

Missed call from Blaise. I phoned back. She answered immediately.

'The zip,' she whispered. 'It's stuck.'

I was sorry to hear it, and told her so.

'Well?' she said. 'I need you to come in and fix it for me.'

'I can't,' I said. 'It's the ladies' changing room. I'm not a lady.'

'I'm a damsel in distress,' said Blaise. 'If you were a gentleman you'd be straight in.'

'Tell you what,' I said. 'Why don't you come out and I'll unzip you on neutral territory.'

'I can't,' said Blaise. 'She'd know.'

'Who'd know?' I said, baffled. 'What would she know?'

'It's two sizes too small,' said Blaise.

'All your dresses are two sizes too small,' I said.

'We've been through this. You buy them so they're the right size when they fit you, after you've given up – '

'I know,' hissed Blaise, sidestepping the C word neatly. 'But I can't help that now. Well?'

'Well what?'

'Please,' said Blaise. 'She'd gloat.'

'I can't go into the ladies,' I said. 'I have history.'

'The Bonnie thing was different,' said Blaise. 'Besides, you were let off with a caution.'

'Look,' I pleaded, 'can't you just phone a friend?'

'I *have* phoned a friend.'

'And?'

'She's in Australia.'

'So?'

A short pause ensued while she formulated her reply. Which, by her standards was curt in the extreme. 'The shop closes in fifteen minutes.' I was about to tell her not to change the subject when she butted in pre-emptively. 'Never mind,' she said. End of call.

At a loose end, I was about to finger the merchandise, marvel at the prices and simultaneously ponder Blaise's next move[24], when she emerged from the changing room; walking with less than her usual grace; possibly experiencing some difficulty with her breathing; her coat buttoned up for a swift exit. She went over to the counter and gave the assistant the full Celtic goddess works. Magisterial. Eyeball to eyeball. No blinking.

'It's perfect,' she gasped. 'I'll take it.'

'I can't understand it,' said Blaise three days later.

We were back in the bedroom. Blaise was – is it

---

[24] I was thinking about the window at the back, not to mention the winching.

possible to be *seething* with distress?

'Well,' I said, 'you *have* been hitting the chocolate a bit recently.'

'No I haven't.'

I may not have captured her tone there, but the temperature dropped several degrees.

'On mature reflection,' I said, 'you're absolutely right. End of subject. Silly me.'

'But I haven't,' repeated Blaise.

'I know,' I said. 'That's what I said.'

'No you didn't. You said 'Well, you *have* been hitting the chocolate a bit recently'.'

'But after that,' I said. 'I qualified my remark by saying the exact opposite.'

'But that's not the point,' said Blaise. 'You think I have.'

'Thought,' I said. 'Past tense. I've seen the error of my ways.'

'I've hardly had any chocolate for months,' said Blaise, inspecting herself closely in the mirror. 'Have I?'

'Well,' I said, 'you may have a slight problem.' I was about to put this in perspective with reference to alcohol, nicotine, narcotics and gambling, but Blaise cut in on my flow before it began.

'That,' she said, 'is where you are so, so wrong. And,' she continued, 'I'll prove it.'

She held her hand out. Much as you would hold your hand out to a not very bright three-year-old. I decided to humour her, and she led me gently to the kitchen.

'This,' she said, 'is the kitchen.'

'I know it's the kitchen,' I said. 'I saw it when we moved in.'

'And these,' she said, 'are the kitchen cupboards.' She opened one and pointed to a modest supply of chocolate. 'Now observe,' said Blaise. She peeled a black bin bag from its parent roll, flapped it open, asked me to hold it – like so – and scooped an armful of chocolate into the bag. A solitary walnut whip remained on the shelf. I looked at it. Blaise looked at it. A moment of truth? To be honest, I quite fancied a walnut whip myself, but perhaps now was not the time. Blaise, with a playful flick of the wrist – Look! I'm not an addict! – fired it after its siblings. She then hoicked the bag over her shoulder and stared defiantly into the middle distance. I may have been blocking the view.

'Happy now?' she said.

'Deliriously so,' I said. 'In fact I expect immediate results. Fancy a quick weigh-in?'

'Cheeky,' she said, and she may have wiggled her posterior as she left the room, heading for the outside bin.

Now it's one thing tossing a hefty bag of chocolate into the bin. It's another thing leaving it there, and Blaise is pretty good at reading my mind on this sort of thing.

'I suppose you'll be setting up CCTV,' she said the following morning as we enjoyed a chocolate-free break. 'You know, make sure a certain person doesn't go foraging in her own bin.'

'Pas du tout,' I said, which I'm pretty sure is French for nonsense, 'because today is bin day and that, unless I'm very much mistaken, will be the bin lorry now.'

Did I detect the merest hint of panic behind Blaise's calm exterior? The flicker of an unguarded eyelid?

Difficult to say, but it was the bin lorry all right. I could hear the bin being rolled, the clatter and thump as it was attached to the back of the lorry, the grind and whoosh as it was lifted and emptied, and – although this may have been my imagination at work – the crunch of a fun-size bag of nut clusters[25] being crushed in the belly of the beast.

I think Blaise may have heard it too. She looked, momentarily, like a six-year-old whose doggy has just been shot. As the bin lorry drove off I stood behind her and placed the healing hand of love on her shoulder. I toyed with the idea of saying her nut clusters had gone to chocolate heaven, but settled on 'You okay?'

'I'm fine,' she said shakily. 'Everything is – everything is fine.'

It wasn't. I could see that. Her words said one thing, her body language another. But at least she didn't run after the lorry.

Now that's what I call progress.

A week later we were on our way to visit Blaise's formidable mother, Isobel, in the idyllic hamlet of Trossach. Isobel is a fine woman in many ways, but she persists with the notion that Blaise is married to her husband, whose name escapes me at present, and that I'm Dr. O'Shaughnessy, General Practitioner, simply because I'm Irish[26].

Blaise jerked the clutch into whatever gear it is you use for hill climbing.

'I haven't lost any weight,' she said through clenched

---

[25] 50% extra free.
[26] The prospect of Isobel's regular check-up filled me with dread. Nudity at that age is not pleasant for either party.

teeth. 'Okay?'

'Sorry,' I said. 'I was only asking. I just thought, you know, three days on lettuce salad.'

'*And* fruit,' said Blaise. '*And* bloody bean bloody stew.'

I'd actually lost a few pounds myself, on what I referred to as the sympathy diet, but I said nothing.

Conversation stalled at this point. We drove on and, maybe it was a bad idea at the time, but I decided to do a spot of spring cleaning. The side pocket. The glove compartment. That sort of thing.

'What on earth are you doing?' said Blaise.

'Just sprucing things up a bit,' I said lightly, as I tucked a wad of tissues into a poly bag.

'Why? Don't you trust me?' she asked.

I put her light-to-moderate snappiness down to the memory of bean stew. In fact there was a large pot of it at home awaiting our return, so I was beginning to feel a little snappy myself.

'Of course I trust you,' I said. 'There's nothing not to trust.'

'Hah,' said Blaise.

We had obviously reached an impasse, but I was committed, so I threw myself into my work. Tissues. Wrappers. One Malteser bag; empty.

'See?' I quipped. 'Result.'

'Yippee,' said Blaise, but I'm not convinced she meant it.

I stuck my hand deep into the back of the glove compartment. What was this? An individually wrapped hazelnut whirl. Cowering in the corner. I pondered my options, then slowly pulled it out. The whirl was public knowledge now. No going back.

'Well?' said Blaise, gripping the steering wheel even more tightly.

I didn't know how to approach this.

'Well what?' I said.

'Just get rid of it,' said Blaise.

'Really?'

Blaise seemed frozen on the road ahead, and I must say I admired her steely resolve. But what to do with the hazelnut whirl? If I placed it on top of the small pile of rubbish it would remain in full view, seducing Blaise like she seduces me. I couldn't toss it out the window; it would take several thousand years to decompose. I wasn't having *that* on my conscience.

So I ate it. While Blaise concentrated on her driving and, as she later confided, on the joys of iceberg lettuce. Did I take pleasure in it? No. It did, however, bring me to a closer understanding of the concept of guilt. Blaise, for her part, said nothing. She might have done given the opportunity, but just as I swallowed the last traces, the front tyre exploded.

The hills looked particularly lovely as I opened the passenger door. The shapes. The colours. The deeply melancholy and yet, somehow, spiritually uplifting *desolation*.

'I'll get the spare,' I said.

'We don't have a spare,' said Blaise. She was using her small voice. The one that disarms criticism. I ignored the signs.

'Of course we have a spare,' I said. 'There's a whole compartment devoted to it in the boot. Trust me. It's a man thing.'

Blaise watched, a strange look in her eyes; as I moved

to the back of the car; as I opened the boot; as I removed the clutter. Several banana skins. Three cagoules. One dusty CD cover[27]. I arranged it all neatly on the grass verge and moved inexorably towards my goal. As the strip of carpet covering the spare wheel flap became visible, Blaise switched to her even smaller voice, so I didn't quite catch what she said next. Possibly 'Pity me'. Or maybe it was 'What have I done?'. No matter. Either would have suited. I braced myself and lifted the flap, a flap which promised, in bold capitals, SPARE WHEEL. Which was perfectly understandable. It was, after all, the spare wheel compartment.

Guess what? No spare wheel. It was, to my astonishment, chock-full, in the most literal sense of the word, of chocolate. Not one cubic centimetre of space remained. If you wished to press the point, you could say it was more suited to chocolate than to spare wheels. But I didn't wish to press the point. 'So where's the spare wheel then?' I said.

Blaise prepared her tiniest voice.

'Under the bed?' she squeaked. Note the implied question mark, as if to suggest that it *might* be under the bed. As if to further suggest that she might not be the person responsible for putting it there. If, indeed, that was where it was. I returned to the passenger seat.

'We have ourselves a problem,' I said.

Blaise pretended to rally. 'I'll phone the breakdown people,' she said, rooting in her bag for her mobile.

I patted her hand. Patronisingly. 'Don't change the subject,' I said, and Blaise knew exactly what I meant.

---

[27] *The Clits – Live in Scrabster*

The 'problem' came up again that evening, as we relaxed over a nice bowl of bean stew at the dining table.

'But the point is I didn't touch *any* of it,' said Blaise. 'That's the *point*.'

'So why was it in the boot?' I asked as I chased a rogue kidney bean around my bowl.

'Aha,' said Blaise. 'Glad you asked me that. It's known as *The Gandhi Strategy*.' She smiled triumphantly. 'I was testing myself.'

I gave up on the bean and put my fork down. 'I see,' I said. 'Perhaps you'd better explain.'

'Gladly,' she said. 'Mahatma Gandhi was – '

'I think we can skip that bit,' I said. 'It's the strategy I'm interested in.'

'Well,' said Blaise, 'the Great Man was reputed to have slept with ladies of the night, vestal virgins, pop starlets of the day and so forth, to test his vows of celibacy.'

'Ah,' I said. '*That* Mahatma Gandhi. I'm with you now. But I hardly think a few kilos of chocolate compares to the lure of the nubile to a hot-blooded celibate icon. Besides, he didn't stick them in the boot.'

Blaise prodded me playfully with her spoon.

'You don't trust me, do you?' she said. 'You think I've got no self-control.'

'In a word?' I said. But I didn't answer my own question. I'd just had a better idea. Why not put this much-vaunted *Gandhi Strategy* to the test? I explained the plan in simple terms. I would sleep on the couch. Blaise would sleep in the bed as usual. Beside her, on the pillow normally reserved for her one true love's head, would rest her spare-wheel chocolate-stash in its entirety. Would it still be there by morning? There, I explained, was the rub.

Night fell. Bedtime beckoned. We went our separate ways. As I closed the bedroom door behind me I experienced an almost imperceptible pang of sexual jealousy. She may have found it easy to swear off *me* for the night. But a catering slab of Turkish Delight?

Twelve minutes later, the rustle of silver foil from the general area of the bedroom suggested the experiment had been a failure. This was serious. Mahatma Gandhi had reputedly lasted nineteen minutes with Miss Rawalpindi 1943 before she was forced to repel his advances, so in a straight Gandhi-Blaise one-to-one, the Great Man would have triumphed by a clear seven minutes. I decided to investigate.

I muted the living room lights and removed my shoes – often the prelude to lovemaking, but not, sad to say, in this case. I opened the bedroom door daintily and snuck in. All was quiet. The soft light from the living room cast a subtle spell over the room. It was all very – what's the word? – *cinematographic*. Blaise laid out like Queen Victoria on her deathbed. But prettier. White nightdress. Hands placed just so. Eyes closed. Regular breathing. Obviously asleep. But hmm, what was this? A slight brown smudge on the otherwise pristine duvet? Could, I supposed, be anything. And this? A sliver of silver foil jutting out from underneath the pillow? Could also be anything.

I was on high alert. Holmes and Watson in one. I won't bother with the internal dialogue, but it was both instructive and dryly humorous. I eased her mouth open with a pinky. Couple of brown fillings? Tut tut. Yet she seemed to be fast asleep. I decided to give her the benefit of the doubt and advise her, in the morning, to consider switching dentists. I turned away and moved lightly back to the door, but as I was leaving I felt an eye opening. Perhaps we spend too much time together, but there it is. I felt it, and once felt it was impossible to unfeel. I turned quickly. The eye was indeed open.

'Inference, Watson?'

'The lady, Holmes, is awake.'

'Why, so she is, Watson. So she deducedly is.'

Blaise later accused me of 'spying on an industrial scale'. A bit harsh, I felt. Besides, as I pointed out, there wouldn't be spies if there was nothing to spy on. Which, in this case, there was.

'So,' I said. 'Not asleep after all.'

Blaise yawned – which she never does – and stretched – which she sometimes does but never in this theatrical way. Then there was her prepared script. 'What? What? Where am I?' That sort of stuff. The bluffer's guide to waking.

'Ah, there you are!' she said, as if just noticing my presence. 'My, but I've had the *sweetest* dream.'

She had chosen her adjective well, but not, perhaps, well enough.

'No you haven't,' I said.

And I was right.

She hadn't.

A few days later, Blaise was unashamedly popping a Belgian truffle into her mouth not two feet from where I sat. From a box of the things. She'd managed to sublimate her need to fit into one of her dresses, but Treasure Mbotze was due to arrive in less than a fortnight for her much-trumpeted International Women's Day event, and the problem was sure to resurface with a vengeance. I knew this. Blaise refused to see a link between chocolate and diet. She needed guidance, and I had just discovered, by sheer fluke, the perfect way to get her to address the issue.

I'd been looking myself up on the internet[28]. Seems I share my name with a present-day slave owner.

'Now *there's* an interesting thing,' I said.

'Hmn?' said Blaise. She was busy studying the box. Belgian truffle or Belgian truffle? Difficult choice. 'What is?' she said.

'The modern day slave owner,' I said, twisting the screen to let her have a look. 'I mean, take a look at this specimen here.'

Blaise waved the screen away in fury. 'These people,' she spluttered, spraying the room with half-digested truffle, 'are beyond contempt. I mean – I mean, the fact that slavery still exists in the modern world! It's – why, it's an *affront to humanity.*'

She went on like this for some time. Articulate. Passionate. No notes. It certainly won me round. 'Pure evil,' she concluded, popping another truffle in her mouth. 'Pure, unadulterated *filth*. So what line of so-called business is he in?'

'*Ah,*' I said. 'You assume he's a he. Could be a she.'

Blaise sighed tragically. 'It gets worse,' she said. 'So okay, what line is *she* in?'

'In this case,' I said reassuringly, 'he *is* a he. Chocolate.'

'Maybe just the one,' said Blaise. 'So what's he in?'

'Chocolate,' I repeated.

Blaise's hand, which had been hovering over the

---

[28] Little hobby of mine. I've always been fascinated by people.

truffle box, hovered no longer. I had her full attention.

'Whatever about its addictive qualities,' I added, as if the idea had just occurred to me, 'I always thought chocolate was ethically above reproach.' I held eye contact. 'You know. *Ethically* speaking.' Note the double use of ethically. She's very big on ethics, Blaise. I knew this. That's why I used it, twice. 'Did you know, for instance, that the chocolate industry feeds the so-called civilised world's lust for chocolate by the subjugation of the indigenous populations of a great many developing countries click here for full list.' An unwieldy sentence I admit, but that's what it said on the screen. I tried to invest it with a hint of righteous outrage and it worked.

'Really?' she said. But there was something about the way she said it. Not 'Really?' but *'Really?'* It sounded a bit premeditated. A bit *forced*.

'You knew that already, didn't you?' I said, and while shamefacedly is a pretty unwieldy adverb, it describes perfectly the way she nodded. Yes, she nodded shamefacedly. All the information on the internet about the dark side of chocolate. She knew it. Yet she continued to eat the stuff. Why?

Why?!

I looked at my beloved, and what I saw shocked me to the deep heart's core. Blaise was an addict. That was why. She would never fit a dress that was two sizes too small for her. She would stand at the end of the bed on International Women's Day, tossing dresses to the four corners of the room, incandescent with distress.

I knew all this. But I didn't say it. No. I didn't have to. I just closed the lid of the laptop and sat there. Blaise sighed deeply. She trembled with emotion as she stood up. She then marched briskly into the kitchen clutching the box of truffles which had caused so much suffering, to so many, so very far away[29]. Moments later I heard the swing bin swinging. I followed Blaise into the kitchen and placed a comforting arm round her still trembling waist.

'What say you,' I said, 'to a nice cup of nettle tea?'

The ethical approach soon broke the twelve minute record for abstention set by Blaise herself and, seven minutes later, left Gandhi's Miss Rawalpindi episode floundering in its wake.[30] But the side effects were painful. Blaise withdrew into herself. She became almost taciturn. I felt I had to say something to ease the pain of withdrawal.

'What say you,' I said, 'to another nice cup of nettle tea?'

Blaise tightened visibly. She said nothing. She did, however, storm into the kitchen and pour the contents of a 250-gram bag of the allegedly calming brew into the bin. The lid swung vigorously back and forth as if to reflect her inner turmoil.

The big psychological breakthrough happened, of all places, at the local supermarket. No names. Pleasingly upmarket if you like that sort of thing. They still sell *Gentlemen's Relish*. But I digress. We were, as I say, at the supermarket. Blaise had been bemoaning her latest

---

[29] Possibly, in this particular case, the Belgian Congo.
[30] Apparently Miss Rawalpindi repelled the Great Man's advances with a swift jab to the ribcage, so technically speaking he remained virgo intactus. His acolytes pounced on this as proof of their hero's virtue. Revisionist historians now regard Miss Rawalpindi 1943 as an icon of early twentieth century feminism.

weigh in. She refused to accept irrefutable scientific evidence that linked chocolate consumption to weight gain or, in its absence, loss. No point pursuing it. She had also been reliably informed by her best friend Faye, an alleged nutritionist, that if you broke a bar of chocolate into tiny pieces the calories fell out. No point pursuing that either; and so, in an effort to prove that I was listening empathetically, I tried to interest her in the lettuce section.

'Look!' I said. '12 different varieties in the one bag. And look! Iceberg lettuce. Oh, and look at those cute little gem lettuces. How often do you see *them*?' Every day, presumably, if you happened to frequent the lettuce section, but I didn't say that either.

Blaise looked disengaged, distrait, bored. Take your pick.

'I've got to get a couple of things,' she said . 'Oh, and we need milk.'

'Here,' I said. 'Let me take the basket.'

'I'm fine,' said Blaise. 'Milk, okay?'

Now all this sounds pretty boring as I read it over. Lettuce? I'll take the basket? Milk, okay? Hardly the stuff of classic drama, particularly if you've seen a lunchtime production of Medea, as we just had.

Back, however, to the lettuce. It has its place in what was about to develop into the makings of a modern Greek tragedy. I was trying to remember what Blaise had asked me to get, but my mind has a habit of wandering on these shopping expeditions, and it was certainly wandering now. I may have been staring at the cake section[31] when Blaise came and parked herself beside me.

---

[31] Cream horns two for the price of three, for those interested in such matters.

As I say, my mind was wandering. I was imagining our lives together over the blissful coming years, and overcome with love and mischief, I patted her gently on the rear.

'Bon-*jour*,' I whispered seductively.

No sooner had I removed my hand than I spotted Blaise lurking in the chocolate section. Several metres from the abovementioned hand. I had patted – unintentionally but try telling that to the judge – the wrong bottom. My whole life passed before me in a split second. Beautiful relationship over. Brutality of the penal system. Forced to become a superannuated rent boy on licenced release. This appalling vista, as I say, unfolded over a split second. Less. A nano-second. The owner of the wrong bottom turned around. She beamed at me.

'Forty years of marriage,' she said, 'and that's my biggest thrill yet. I'll take what's left of the cream horns.'

The cream horn bit was said to the man behind the counter. She had more important things on her mind than a piddling case of sexual harassment. I had been given a last minute reprieve. I felt *fantastic*. Blaise reappeared with her basket. In pride of place, I noticed, lettuce. Iceberg. Little Gem. Boil in the blessèd bag. And, tucked away discreetly under this feast of foliage, two large slabs of ethically correct *Fruit and Nut*.

'*You* look happy,' said Blaise. Phew, I thought. I'm in the clear. I thanked a non-existent deity and danced a metaphorical jig. Cream Horn Woman took possession of a large packet of her pastries of choice, and as she turned to go she gave me a conspiratorial wink.

Blaise looked totally confused. 'What was that all

about?' she said.

Guilt was written all over the deep contours of my face. I couldn't tell a lie. 'I patted her on the bottom,' I gulped as we headed towards the tills, 'and said hello in French.' I was about to contextualise the situation, with specific reference to the subconscious workings of the brain, as my co-respondent, oblivious to the unfolding drama, waddled laboriously away. Blaise watched her go with an expression of unbearable sadness on her lovely face. I felt terrible.

'I didn't mean it,' I said. 'It was totally involuntary. I thought it was you!'

'I know,' said Blaise sounding, suddenly, terminally tearful.

Blaise excused herself. She'd forgotten something apparently. I looked again at the woman. She was *uber*-large. With matching bottom. I suddenly understood. I marched resolutely after Blaise. I knew exactly where I'd find her. She was placing two large slabs of ethically correct *Fruit and Nut* back on Special Offers. Her body bent with sorrow, I heard a tiny wail, like a lost soul from the twelfth circle of hell.

'Help me-e-e!'

For the next two weeks Blaise was a chocolate-free zone. The morning of the visit from Treasure Mbotze she excitedly threw her wardrobe door open. All that abstinence! She could wear her choice of dresses. But it didn't stop her fishing for compliments.

'Oh, I don't know what to wear,' she said. 'Decisions, decisions. Treasure will be stunning as always and I'll be – .'

'Lovely,' I said. 'You'll be absolutely lovely. You've lost – what? – almost two pounds. That's – why, that's almost the size of a two-pound box of chocolates. Well *done*.' I should have stopped there, but I wanted to spur her on to greater things. 'But,' I continued, 'and it's a big but – '

Huge mistake. The English language is full of hidden traps for the unwary. Blaise almost crumpled.

'Shame on you,' she gasped, glancing at her rear view in the full-length mirror. 'Shame on you.' She paused for tragic effect. 'Anyway, I can't stand around here being humiliated, much as I'd love to. I'm off in two minutes.'

I was formulating an apology for the But-word that was craven but credible, when the doorbell rang. Dan. Just happened to be passing. Good timing, frankly. I ushered him in. Moments later, Blaise came out of the bedroom looking pretty damned gorgeous.

'Lovely dress,' said Dan. 'Let me guess. Lambswool?'

'Very good,' said Blaise, giving us a playful twirl. 'I'm impressed.'

'Thought so,' said Dan. 'Maybe you should hand wash it next time.' Blaise froze. Dan, who didn't understand the concept of the warning signal vis-à-vis women, pressed on. 'I had a lambswool shirt once. Stuck it in the machine. Total disaster. Had to give it to little Declan.'

Blaise cracked down the middle and disintegrated. Not literally, but she might as well have done. She scrabbled round in her handbag for any stray chocolate and left, moments later, traumatised. I knew Blaise. She'd be straight round to the corner shop. Back to square one. When Blaise relapses, she relapses big.

'Did I say something?' said Dan.

'I think you probably did,' I said.

His moustache looked upset. His eyes may have betrayed an inner turmoil. Difficult to tell with Dan. But possible. So I told him everything. Man to man. Blaise. Chocolate. Obsession with dress size. More chocolate.

'Addiction,' I said. 'There's no other word for it, and it's tearing us *apart*, Dan. *Tearing us apart.*'

'I see,' said Dan. 'I see.' He was thinking deeply. For Dan. 'Now hold on a minute,' he said. 'Remember that rock star. You know the one.' I didn't. 'Leather trousers. Fly buttons on the outside. Wispy hair. Pretty obnoxious all round, and big, I mean *grand style* into the drink-stroke-drugs. Tries everything. Rehab, the lot. Nothing works. So anyway, her long-suffering husband gathers together every syringe, bottle and ash tray in the obligatory rock legend mansion. Piles them up on the lawn. Gathers her nearest and dearest from round the globe. Private jet job. Legend arrives home. Huge stash in full public view. Humiliated, but it works. Cured.' Dan paused for a moment's wistful reflection. 'Bit of a tragic coda. She discovers Scientology. All efforts to get her back on the drugs fail miserably. Her husband dies a broken man.'

'So what are you suggesting?' I said. 'We try this on Blaise?'

'Ah no,' said Dan. 'Bit harsh.' He paused again. 'On the other hand,' he said, 'might be worth a try. How long will she be gone?'

'She's introducing Treasure Mbotze at the Women's Library. You know. The novelist.'

'Ah yes,' said Dan. 'Big fan. Big fan.'

'Thing is,' I said, 'she'll be gone for a while.'

'In that case,' said Dan, 'let's get cracking.' He fondled his moustache for a meditative moment. 'Or maybe not. Bit harsh?'

I was suddenly resolute. 'No,' I said. 'It isn't.' It was time to deal with the problem head on. Lance the metaphorical boil. No half measures. Blaise and I would grow old together and all her dresses would fit. This wouldn't happen by itself.

Dan rubbed his hands together like the foreman he may once have been.

'Right,' he said. 'First things first. Might take a bit of time to contact the family, so who is there?'

'Tough one,' I said. 'There's her mother, I suppose.'

'Not too sure about that,' said Dan. 'Women stick together. What about her husband?'

'Husband?' I said.

Dan looked vaguely haunted. Could have been my icy stare. 'I thought she had a husband,' he said.

'Ex-husband, Dan. Ex.'

'Even better,' said Dan. 'No love lost, eh?'

I may have snorted with contempt. 'I'm not phoning her ex-husband.'

'Protocol, eh?' said Dan. 'Gotcha.'

I was about to suggest we get cracking when I was suddenly struck by a thought. 'Slight problem,' I said. 'The bit about piling all the stuff on the lawn.'

'What about it?'

'We don't have a lawn.'

'A detail,' said Dan. 'The lawn is symbolic. Next step. Time to gather the evidence. Empty wrappers. Secret stashes. That sort of thing. So. Where to start.'

Where indeed? The flat was small, the possibilities endless. Blaise loves books, for instance, so we checked the bookshelves in tandem. With particular reference, Dan insisted, to hollowed out Bibles.

'We don't do Bibles,' I said.

'Torah? Book of Mormon? Koran?' I gave him a look. 'Complete Works of L. Ron Hubbard?' I gave him another look. 'Fine,' he said. 'I'll check the bedroom, you check – '

'You won't check the bedroom,' I said. 'The bedroom is our private place. We have things in there.'

'Gotcha,' said Dan. '*You* check the bedroom. I'll check behind the cistern. It's where the Mafia hide their guns. What things?'

'Things,' I said.

'Well,' said Dan. 'As long as you don't have things behind the cistern.'

'No, Dan,' I said. 'We don't have things behind the cistern. Or in the kitchen.'

'Fine,' said Dan. 'Cistern. Kitchen.'

We regrouped some minutes later. Nothing.

'What about this room here?' said Dan.

'That's Blaise's study,' I said. 'It's locked.'

Dan tried the door. 'So it is.'

I pointed at the sign on the door. No entry. With accompanying footnote[32].

'It's a no-go area,' I said.

'Is it now?' said Dan. '*Is* it now indeed?' He pointed through the door. 'There's your stash,' he said. 'Trust me. I have an instinct for these things.'

'I don't have a key,' I said. 'And she's hidden the

---

[32] Not to mention footnotes on footnotes, as previously footnoted.

spare. There's no way we're getting in there.'

'Watch this,' said Dan. He felt above the door jamb and produced a key. 'I'll say this for her,' he said. 'She's got *you* worked out.'

He breathed on the key and polished it with his sleeve. I held my hand out for it. He shrugged and passed it over. I slipped it into the keyhole and turned it slowly and with great deliberation. I describe the actions because I was breaking the unwritten code. As I braced myself and pushed the door open, my mobile went.

Blaise! But how could she possibly know?! I decided to take the call – it would all come out later anyway – and was about to blurt out a stuttering apology when Blaise blurted out ahead of me.

'I've split my dress,' she blurted. 'What am I going to *do*? Sorry. Got to go.'

'It's very small,' said Dan. What? Had Dan been listening in? He may have caught my expression. 'The study,' he said. 'It's very small.' Ah, the study. He had a point. It *was* very small. 'Still,' he said, 'I expect she manages to fit.'

'Put like that,' I said, 'yes. She does.'

It took a mere matter of minutes to comb the place. Drawers. Folders. The usual paraphernalia of a compact office space.

Her latest slim volume sat on the desk. Dan insisted on checking it for after dinner mints. Nothing.

'Hold on,' said Dan. 'What's this?' He knelt on the floor, scrabbled behind the desk, and stood up holding a mouldy green Malteser. We took it next door as evidence, placed it in a saucer on the living room table, and examined it for a long moment.

'Don't knock it,' said Dan. 'It's a start.'

'No, it isn't,' I said. 'We've looked everywhere. It's a finish.'

'What about the cellar?' said Dan.

'What cellar?' I said. 'There *is* no cellar.'

'All these houses have cellars,' said Dan. He stroked his moustache meditatively. 'Call it a hunch.'

To be fair to Dan, he seemed to have a good strike rate on the hunch front, so we shoved the furniture to one side, and yanked the carpet up to reveal a rectangular hatch fitted neatly into well-seasoned floorboards. The sight of such craftsmanship was like a magical trip to a bygone century. It all felt so – what's the word I'm looking for? – *old*. We prised the hatch open to reveal a rickety set of steps leading down to the flat's dank netherworld. I located a torch in mounting excitement and we negotiated the musty smell and cobwebs till we reached rubble-strewn earth.

Dan was suddenly alert. 'Over there. Torch.'

I shone the torch on the farthest corner of the cellar. What had we here? Row upon row of dust-strewn chocolate boxes awaiting Blaise's return? No. A long-abandoned wine cellar. Row upon row of dust-and-debris-caked bottles of manifestly ancient vintage, left to ferment undisturbed by a previous owner for reason or reasons unknown. Dan extracted a bottle and blew the dust off. He grabbed the torch excitedly and shone it, equally excitedly, on the label.

'Look at that *year*,' he gushed. 'We've hit the veritable mother lode, amigo. Assuming it's kept its fizz.' Before I could remonstrate he'd pulled the gold foil from the rim and yanked the cork from the bottle. 'Whoops, no glasses,' he yelped as the cork plopped out and a gush of foam splattered the cellar walls. He put the bottle to his lips and stopped the flow with his mouth. 'Now that,' he said, 'is what I call a fine wine.' He passed the bottle over, his moustache glistening with froth.

'No, thank you,' I said. I sounded, to these ears anyway, stern and unyielding – a bit like Mahatma Gandhi in the opening eighteen minutes. But like Mahatma Gandhi I succumbed. I may have mentioned elsewhere my own difficulties getting the balance right with alcohol. The incident at the tercentenary of the annual Porridge Tossing Championship at Inverkeithing springs to mind. Sadly, once these things are plastered all over the internet it's impossible to get them off[33]. But a few discreet bubbles surely wouldn't hurt. Besides, Dan can be very persuasive.

I took a gentle, exploratory sip and found that it was good. No, better than good. Found that it was *excellent*. Dan prised the bottle from me and took another deep slurp. He complimented the wine again on its essential wine-ness and passed the bottle back. We passed it back and forth in silence, a silence I eventually broke with what I took to be words of profound wisdom.

'Now that,' I hiccuped, 'is what you call a fine wine. And so do I, Dan,' I hiccuped again, 'so do I.'

'So where's this chocolate, then?' slurred Dan.

'There *is* no chocolate, Dan,' I tittered. 'Don't you see? There *is* no chocolate.'

'But what about chocolates on the lawn?' said Dan.

'Everything is falling into place,' I chortled. 'There *is* no lawn.'

---

[33] Upwards of three million hits on that one, I'm told. I've turned down offers to tour.

'Well I must say that's excellent news,' said Dan. 'No chocolates, no lawn. Job, you might say, done.'

I was about to congratulate him on his profound profundity when sounds from above choked the words in my mouth. A door closing. Footsteps. Blaise's voice from the hall.

'Hell – '

She had begun to say hello, but something had stopped her. I hiccuped and gulped at the same time, plucked the empty bottle from Dan's reluctant hand, and slid it back on the shelf. It really had been an excellent vintage, but to each action there is an equal and opposite reaction, and I was pretty sure we were set to experience the latter.

I made my way up the rickety stairs and blinked into daylight. Books everywhere, chairs strewn about the floor, the carpet resting on the sofa, and there, in the middle of chaos, Blaise. In a stunning African dress. Beside her stood Treasure Mbotze in another stunning African dress. Under normal circumstances I would have commented on how *fantastic* they looked, but these circumstances were anything but normal. Blaise's eyes were fixed on the mouldy green Malteser. I sniggered. Not a good idea in the circumstances, but to be fair it was involuntary.

'There's a perfectly good explanation for everything,' I hiccuped.

'I know that,' said Blaise. 'I just don't know what it is.'

This, for some reason, set Dan off as he clambered through the hatch.

'*Yet*,' he snorted. 'You don't know what it is *yet*. But you will when he tells you all.' He waved a conductor's hand in my direction. 'You have the floor, Maestro.'

Blaise had taken her eyes off the Malteser and was now focused on her open study door.

'Thing is,' I said. Said? Hiccuped? Probably a bit of both. 'I was just telling Dan here how small your study is.'

'That's it,' said-stroke-giggled Dan. 'That's exactly it.' He looked at me. 'Is it?'

'So I said, what about converting the cellar? Isn't that right? Dan?'

Dan focused in. 'I cannot tell a lie,' he said.

I took up the story from there. 'We were hoping to have it finished before you got back.' I studied Blaise to see how this was going down. Let's call her inscrutable at this stage. So I turned to Treasure Mbotze.

Treasure beamed at me. 'You've found yourself a good man, Blaise,' she said. 'And a good man is the pearl beyond price.'

I took to Treasure immediately. 'Big fan,' I said. 'Big fan.'

'Me too,' giggled Dan.

'And what do you think of your lovely wife's dress?' said Treasure. 'She had a bit of an accident, but it turns out she's precisely the same size as me.' She turned to Blaise. 'All I can say is, it's lucky you're so petite.'

Blaise blushed happily. I giggled happily. I could have kissed Treasure, because once Blaise blushes happily she's incapable of unblushing. The mood had shifted on its axis.

'That really is excellent news about the new study space,' said Blaise. 'But before you go back to work, I think this calls for a celebration. Pity there's no wine in the house.'

'Funny you should mention that,' said Dan. 'Because I think,' he waved dramatically at the hatch, 'I may have spotted a wine cellar in the cellar.'

'Fancy that,' said Blaise. 'Anything else down there?' Her eyes were now fixed on me. 'Like, for instance – '

'No chocolate,' said Dan. 'This,' he said, holding up the mouldy Malteser, 'was found elsewhere.'

I looked at Blaise. Blaise looked at me. Dan looked at both of us and decided, wisely, not to get further involved.

'Wine,' he said, swaying over to the trapdoor and disappearing slowly from view down the rickety steps. Legs. Body. Moustache.

Treasure rooted in her bag. 'Speaking of Maltesers,' she said, 'I almost forgot!' She produced a huge box of chocolates and thrust them, beaming, at Blaise. 'From Senegal. Organic. Fairtrade. Handmade by my people. A little thank you for *everything*.'

Blaise may have cast a pleading glance in my direction, but I was too busy embracing my new role as project manager. It would take some time to adapt the cellar to the needs of a beautiful, if menopausal, poet, however, so I decided to postpone commencement of work, at least till our guests were gone. I cleared a space on the sofa and motioned Blaise and Treasure to pray be seated.

They settled in as Dan made his way back up the rickety steps, merrily whistling an old Gaelic drinking song. Treasure beamed at Blaise. Blaise beamed at me as she opened the substantial lid of the ethical chocolate box with an ease born of many years practice.

'I'm not really supposed to,' she giggled. 'Still, I don't suppose one will do any harm.'

And she was right. It didn't.

Twice a Catholic

> I proposed to her on bended knee. She accepted, of course, as I can be damned attractive when I put my mind to it.

I closed the book with a sigh. Good timing, as Dan had just spotted me at my regular bench in the Botanics, nestled midway between the herb and rose gardens.

'What's the book?' he said, striding manfully over.

It was, in fact, the latest Lizzie Borden. But I wasn't prepared to share my newly acquired taste for romantic fiction with a male friend. 'Plato,' I said, hastily tucking it into my pocket. 'You know. The Poetics.'

'Pink cover,' he said as he sat down beside me. 'Interesting marketing strategy. I wonder who *that's* aimed at?'

I didn't rise to the bait, because that's what it was. Besides, I was suddenly lost in my own thoughts. Of all the writers in all the world, why had I chosen *Plato*?

Dan tapped his fingers on the bench behind me. 'Funny thing,' he said. 'You normally associate pink covers with romantic fiction.'

'I wouldn't know about that,' I said. 'I'm not a marketing strategist.'

'Whereas you normally associate *Plato*,' he continued, choosing to ignore me, 'with ancient Greek philosophy. And,' he paused here to prolong his little moment, 'you normally associate *The Poetics* with Aristotle. But who am I? Who, in a word, am I?'

He was toying with me. In his own mind he had already won this particular mental joust and was enjoying a pre-emptive gloat.

'There's a very simple explanation for the pink,' I said, as if explaining to a child. 'You see, Plato was the first great romantic. You'll know the story.' He didn't. Neither, for that matter, did I, but you don't admit ignorance to the Dans of this world and in any case, I was more than happy to make it up. 'According to Plato,' I continued, 'humans originally had four arms, four legs and a two-faced head. They also had two sets of genitalia, but we won't go into that. Somewhere along the line, they became arrogant, so Zeus – '

'Are we talking about Zeus the God here,' interrupted Dan, 'or Zeus the world's tallest dog, who died in Michigan just days before his sixth birthday.[34]'

'Don't be flip, Dan,' I counter-interrupted. 'Humans became arrogant, so Zeus decided to split them in two. Two arms; two legs; one head; ditto on the genital front. Pretty much what we're left with today. But here's the twist. The two halves, thus divided, wander off to live separate lives – '

' – of quiet desperation,' said Dan.

'Possibly,' I said. 'But see what happens. They get lonely. Each half pines for its other half. They wander the earth, pining and searching, which, from Zeus' point of view, keeps them out of mischief; and when they do find each other they know deep down it was meant to be. They know they're' – and this is where Lizzie's title came in handy – '*Soul Mates*.'

Dan's eyes misted over. 'You mean,' he said, 'like us?'

---

[34] Sad case, but not pertinent to this particular narrative. Another time, perhaps.

'Well,' I said, 'I was thinking more me and Blaise.'

'Oh, right,' said Dan. 'Take your point.' There followed a short pause while he wrestled with his thoughts. 'One *slight* problem, though.'

'Problem?'

'With the soul bit.'

'I don't follow.'

'Well,' said Dan, 'I'm willing to bet you've been baptised.'

'And?'

'You have, haven't you?'

'Your point?'

'*Ipso facto,*' said Dan, 'your soul is not your own. The legal owner is the Catholic church.' I hadn't thought of that. I did now. Dan had landed a low blow, and it hurt. Not that he noticed. 'You see what I did there?' he said. 'I've entered a note of soul doubt.' He chortled happily. 'Soul doubt,' he repeated. 'It's sort of a – '

'A pun, Dan,' I said. 'It's a pun. Very droll.'

'Thanks,' said Dan. 'Appreciate that.' He fell silent for a while, deep in his own thoughts. Then he got up to leave. 'Soul doubt,' he tittered softly as he wandered slowly off.

I glanced around in a state of what might best be described as languorous agitation. I hate puns above all attempts at low humour, but did Dan have a point? Was my soul not my own? I watched in melancholy anguish as nature took its course. Butterflies fluttering; bees a-buzzing; a couple of dragonflies locked together in a circular dance; and all around me, it seemed, flowers, plants, even the brute bushes of the field, cross-pollinating in that age-old mating ritual called love.

And I in the midst of all; alone, alone, alone.

I wrote to the Pope as soon as I got home. The exact wording must remain forever private, but it was brief and to the point. Short paragraph about love for Blaise. Brief biog of Blaise with particular reference to religious non-affiliation, but probable Protestant background if her hellfire-and-brimstone mother was anything to go by. Mention, with recommended reading list, of Platonic concept of Soul Mate as referred to above. Request for return of soul. Fond regards to the Curia. Yours Et Cetera.

I was happy with the tone, ending with a matey PS: Where *do* you buy those hats? I also felt sure the Pope would appreciate that at the age I was at the time of the original transaction[35], and given the recent trauma of being physically separated from my mother, I'd been in no fit state to make an informed decision on anything, least of all the ownership of my immortal soul.

I kept all this well hidden from my – literally – other half for obvious reasons, but after I posted it I may have been unsettled for some time. Our trip to the local greengrocer was untypically devoid of romance and, as we got ready for bed that night, I noticed Blaise giving me her concerned look.

'Anything you'd like to talk about?' she said.

'Not especially, no. Why?'

'It's just that, well, you've been acting strangely recently. Well, more strangely than usual, put it like that.'

My non-verbal response may have been furtive, shifty, sly – take your pick. I ducked under the covers

---

[35] Nought, as I recall.

and peered out.

'This afternoon, for instance,' she continued, 'did you or did you not bless yourself as we – shall we say *negotiated* that lingerie shop on Great Western Road?'

This sounded remarkably specific. I sat up. 'What lingerie shop?'

'You know very well what lingerie shop.'

I did. *Seduction*. Good name. It gets straight to the point. I wasn't aware of blessing myself as we passed, and that was worrying in itself. I ducked back under the covers, and this time I didn't peer back out. End of conversation. But my mind continued to grapple with the subject, so I exercised the rigorous mental discipline of the dedicated ascetic and thought about *Seduction* instead.

I'd kept my Papal correspondence a secret from Blaise because I feared, not her righteous wrath but her gentle ribbing. Every morning I listened for the tell-tale plop of the Papal response on the mat. Blaise was usually in her study at this point, trying to crack that elusive rhyme for orange or whatever it is she gets up to in there, so all it required, on my part, was eternal vigilance; and one morning, some days later, it arrived. Plop. Double plop actually. It was not alone.

Best vellum. Papal seal. To borrow a phrase from the sporting world, the boy done good. I popped the letter in my pocket and returned to the living room. Blaise stuck her head round the door of her study and peered at me over her reading glasses.

'Was that the post?' she said.

'Just a catalogue from *Seduction*,' I said, handing it

over. 'My treat.'

'That it?'

I could feel the Pope's letter burning a hole in my pocket. 'Yup.'

'It's just, well, I thought I heard more than one plop.' She maintained eye contact. It was almost as if she knew. But how could she? Unless it was some Protestant thing.

'Could have been an incoming email,' I suggested.

'Right,' said Blaise. 'That'll be it.'

She may have toyed with the idea of some good-natured teasing, but decided to concentrate on rhyming that orange instead. Phew. I retired to the bathroom, locked the door, waited till I heard the tickle of her laptop keys. I then retrieved the Pope's envelope, broke the wax seal and removed the letter. Moments later I was on the phone to Dan.

'I've just had a letter from the Pope,' I said. 'Bit of a problem. I was hoping you'd give me the benefit of your great learning.'

Excellent psychology. I could hear him preening himself at the other end.

'Can it wait?' he said. 'I'm on a double shift.'

'Not to worry,' I said. 'I'll ask around. There's sure to be – '

More excellent psychology. I could hear him bristling at the other end.

'I can make seven at the Oran Mór,' he said. 'It'll have to be a quick one.'

End of conversation. I'd just put the phone down when Blaise's door opened.

'Mother's just phoned,' she said. 'She took a short cut over Trossach links on her buggy and she's bunkered on the Glorious Twelfth. We'll have to go over.'

'Ah,' I said. 'I've arranged to meet Dan at the Oran Mór. Bit of man to man stuff.'

'When exactly?' said Blaise.

'Seven.'

'Bit tight,' said Blaise, 'but I'm sure we'll make it back.'

'He's a bit pushed for time,' I said. 'Can't it wait?'

'I can't just leave her out overnight,' said Blaise. 'She's eighty six. She might rust. You'll have to come. I'll need your help to hoick her out.'

Blaise pulled to a halt outside the Oran Mór just on seven. Isobel was tucked up in bed. I was on time. Blaise was going to take the car back to the flat, freshen up and meet me in half an hour for a drink. Perfect. I'd see Dan on his own, we'd discuss the letter discreetly at our leisure, Blaise would arrive, have a glass of wine, perhaps two, and who knew what pleasures lay ahead when the love of my life was a little tipsy and I was a little – but let's draw a discreet veil over the latter part of the evening. It was 7pm. There was work to be done.

As Blaise drove off I was amazed to see, outside the main entrance, this:

God Is Not Dead
BBC4 Change of Heart Lecture by Leading Eugenicist
Professor Richard Crabbit
Free Admission
All Faiths and None

Was this the same Professor Crabbit who once said 'God is dead. I should know. I killed him.'?

It was a sign. Literally. Crabbit, it seemed, was a turncoat. As I entered the cavernous bar of the venue I spotted the Learned Professor himself, sitting alone at a table, furiously poring over his notes. I recognised him from that huge domed head. The eyebrows which brooked no argument. The apoplectic face, permanently about to explode.

Unfortunately, the only free table was next to him. He seemed to have that effect on people. I sat gingerly down, and Dan arrived moments later. I handed the letter over. Dan examined the Papal seal approvingly. It oozed privilege, and you've got to give it to the Vatican: they don't stint on the envelopes. Dan seemed to increase in stature just holding the thing. I decided to leave him to it and went to the bar to get him 'a swift half'. Dan sat gingerly on my seat, opened the letter and began to read.

It took a while to get served, what with the rabbis, imams, pastors, reverends, mullahs, vicars and priests all shouting orders at the overworked staff. Add to that a smattering of non-denominationals[36] and you had the makings of a full house.

I took Dan's drink over to the table. He took a sip, wiped his moustache, then stroked it for an interminable time before he spoke. He placed the letter on the table and pressed his fingers together meditatively.

'Problem is,' he said, 'my Latin's a bit rusty.'

'Mine too,' I said. 'Mine too.'

We were about to sink into contemplative silence when an elderly man with the soutane and tri-cornered

---

[36] Possibly plain-clothes atheists come to bury their leader.

hat of the Catholic cleric coughed politely and leaned across from Professor Crabbit's table. The professor, who hadn't spotted him yet, pored on oblivious.

'I am torn between my vows of humility,' said the cleric, 'and the desire to put my years of study to some practical use.' He leaned further in. 'I speak fluent Latin,' he said, indicating the letter now lying on the table. 'Perhaps if I may?'

Dan and I exchanged a look. Was this yet another case of the Lord moving in mysterious ways his wonders to perform? It was certainly oddly serendipitous. I passed the letter over.

The cleric read contemplatively. His brow furrowed. He tutted softly. 'He is so wrong, Lord. So, so wrong.' The words came in a subdued whisper of almost unbearable melancholy, so much so that I felt, somehow, as if I was intruding on private grief. He then made eye contact again and, to my astonishment, tore the letter, meticulously, into tiny pieces.

'Let me tell you a little story,' he said, pushing the pieces into a tidy pile. 'When I was a young man, *many* years ago now, I loved a woman. Much as you, dear child, do now. I was Catholic. She was, well, let us say we lived on opposite sides of the sectarian divide. The barbed wire of the heart. I, sadly, was an immovable object, she a fixed position in the firmament. Our love was doomed from the start. Tristan, if you will, and Isolde. I' – he stifled a sigh and continued – 'took holy orders shortly afterwards. She – well, who knows? Our paths have never crossed from that day to this.' He leaned towards me and became suddenly animated. 'You, however, have your whole life ahead of you, young man. As for this' –

he moved the pieces of the Pope's letter around on the table – 'The Holy Father may be infallible,' he said, 'but that doesn't make him right.' He looked around to check that no-one was listening in. 'Would I be right in saying you're a non-believer?'

I glanced over at Professor Crabbit. He seemed preoccupied with his notes, but you never knew. As an ex-non-believer he might well have the zeal of the convert, and he certainly looked capable of violence in defence of his god.

I dropped my voice to a whisper.

'At present, Father Tristan,' I said, 'yes. Yes I am.'

Tristan fixed me with his doleful, unblinking gaze. He, too, lowered his voice.

'The very existence of the Catholic Church,' he said, 'is predicated on unquestioning belief. If you don't believe, then your soul, assuming you have one, is your own.'

I worked this through in my mind as Dan played distractedly with his glass. It made perfect sense in a nonsensical sort of way. Bit like the Holy Trinity. Or the Virgin Birth. Or, well, all of it actually. Suddenly I felt liberated. My soul soared. There. I had it from a man of the cloth. My soul was my own. There was no impediment to Blaise and I being united together forever. Two heads. Four arms. The other stuff. Tristan clenched his priestly hands with transparent emotion.

'Fly to her!' he beseeched. 'Fly to her!'

That wouldn't be necessary as she was dropping in later, but I didn't tell Tristan that. Let him live the romantic dream. I was about to thank him for his kind assistance when Professor Crabbit raised his magnificent head.

'How very Jesuitical.'

Tristan beamed at him. 'That's not altogether surprising, Professor. I *am* a Jesuit, and I must say I'm greatly looking forward to your little talk. Now if you'll kindly excuse me, I really must micturate in preparation. The waterworks are not what they were.'

He prised himself slowly from his seat, looked nervously skyward, then turned back towards me. 'We haven't had this conversation,' he whispered. Then he creaked slowly off.

'Dying breed,' muttered Professor Crabbit. 'Sooner the better.'

Well, I thought, his recent conversion certainly hasn't mellowed him. His newfound God must be strictly Old Testament.

Dan looked confused. 'Micturate?' he said.

Professor Crabbit cackled. 'Piss.'

'Nice word,' said Dan. 'Micturate. Anyway, best be off. Work beckons.' He drained his glass and stood up. 'By the way.' He pulled a luminous pink book from his pocket. 'The latest Lizzie Borden,' he said, slapping it on the table. '*Soul Mates*. Hope you like it as much as I did.' He raised his hand to the professor. 'God bless,' he said. Then he was gone.

Professor Crabbit scowled at the book. 'Bit of an intellectual, are we?'

There was something about his tone. An implied criticism. I patted the book protectively. 'Big fan,' I said. 'Big fan.'

'More fool you,' sneered the professor. 'From my research on the subject it's clear that romantic love is simply a chemical reaction to certain stimuli, and can be bracketed with alcohol, religion and skunkweed as the opiate of the masses.'

'But surely,' I said, 'your recent conversion – '

'Conversion?' He threw his head back and laughed. 'Conversion? Ha! I have those idiots fooled. If God doesn't exist, which he patently *doesn't*, then he can't very well be dead.'

I was thinking 'How very Jesuitical' when Blaise sat down in the seat vacated by Dan.

'He?' she said.

'Pardon?' barked Crabbit.

'I said 'He?',' said Blaise. 'You know. As in he, she, it.'

Professor Crabbit's eyebrows bristled. 'Your point?'

'If God doesn't exist,' said Blaise evenly, 'he can't very well be a he, now can he?'

'Semantics,' barked the professor.

End of subject, I thought. Blaise will have the good sense to leave it there. No point arguing with these people.

'I see,' she said. 'So even a non-existent deity is masculine. How very patriarchal.'

'Double semantics and poppycock.'

I was about to butt in here – change the subject if possible – but it was then that the learned Prof took note of Blaise's essential femaleness. Her – let's call it *beauty*. Once a eugenicist, I suppose. He was probably thinking about the Master Race – propagation of. So he changed the subject himself.

'By the way,' he leered gruffly, 'call me Dick.'

Blaise gave him her sweetest, most disarming smile.

'I was getting to that bit.'

The professor may have caught an edge. Difficult

to tell. At any rate, he made his excuses, gathered up his notes and stormed upstairs. Father Tristan, who had finished micturating, followed him slowly up. He seemed to be talking to himself as he made the ascent, and I could just about make out his words over the buzz of the crowd.

'Fly to her!' he entreated. 'Fly to her!'

Blaise squeezed my hand. 'Fancy going up?' she said. 'Could be fun.'

I tossed the Pope's confetti in the air and got down on one knee. It could indeed be fun, I thought. A whole mess of fun.

But first there was the small matter of the proposal.

Entwined

I opened the door on the living room. It was in total chaos. Clothes everywhere; pink champagne; and in the midst of all, Blaise. Lost in her own world. What I call *World of Full-length Mirror.*

'Scoot,' said Bonnie, waving a pair of hair straighteners at me. 'You're not supposed to see the bride before the wedding.'

'What about Dan?' I said. Dan, dressed in his finest black suit and propping up the mantelpiece, grinned at me over a glass of pink champagne.

'He's not the groom, Dad,' said Bonnie.

'Right,' I said. 'Point taken.'

'Tell you what,' said Bonnie, taking the glass from Dan and steering us both gently towards the front door, 'Why don't you two just head for the Registry Office and we'll see you there.'

'Are you quite sure you trust us?' I said. There was a tone there. Bonnie chose to ignore it.

'The Registry Office is just across the park, Dad. You have three hours to do a five minute walk. What could possibly go wrong?'

Blaise may have stifled a laugh. Difficult to say. I, on the other hand, was in no mood for flippancy.

'It's nineteen minutes, actually,' I said. 'I've timed it. Twice. The ceremony starts at 2.30, so technically speaking' – in the interests of scrupulous accuracy I referred to my watch – 'that gives us precisely two hours and fifty seven minutes.'

I looked to Dan for moral support. *You showed 'em, buddy*. That sort of thing. He shuffled sheepishly.

'Maybe we'd better get going,' he mumbled.

'Very well then,' I said. 'See you there.'

I addressed this to my betrothed, but Blaise said nothing. She was obviously taking this not-seeing-the-bride thing seriously. Add that to her born again virginity since the banns had been posted and it was turning into quite a tough buildup. I ushered Dan out and was just about to close the door when Blaise broke her silence. 'What could possibly go wrong?' We left to the sound of raucous female laughter. Personally, I failed to see the joke.

Precisely three minutes later we crossed the road to take the shortcut through the Botanic Gardens.

'I do love a spring wedding,' said Dan, as we entered the tree-lined path.

'Me too,' I said. 'Me too. Yet is there not something lovely about this time of year as well? Late September. Sun struggling over the rooftops. Not to get too poetic about it, but russet leaves bathing the paths in an autumny sort of way.'

'Put like that,' sighed Dan. 'I don't know, though. At my age it sort of reminds me of – '

'Dan,' I said. 'This is a wedding. It may be the wrong time to say this, but the undertaker outfit was a mistake.'

'Okay,' said Dan, as an old man hobbled past leaning heavily on his stick. 'It's just, you know. September.'

'I know, Dan. I know. September.'

We drifted into melancholy silence as we exited the Botanics. Across the road the doors of the Oran Mór were open wide and inviting.

'Just the one?' said Dan.

'Just the none, Dan,' I said.

'Only joshing.'

I said nothing. He wasn't. I ushered him past the entrance and we strolled along the Byres Road like two ageing outlaws. The townsfolk fell silent as we passed. Time slowed. I savoured the taste of imaginary chaw tobaccy as I checked the rooftops for the glint of sunlight on gun-metal. Dan probably did too. Old habits. Only two hours thirty eight minutes to go. Would we make it? I chawed my baccy and kept my own counsel. My steely grey eyes gave nothing away. *Sure* we would.

I'm trying to inject a bit of drama into proceedings here, but sometimes, just sometimes, everything works out for the best; and while we're on the subject, what's wrong with a narrative arc that moves from a happy beginning, via a happy middle, to a happy ever after? Not wishing to get on my high horse or anything, but the world is full of misery, woe, tragedy; heartache, doom and gloom. War. Pestilence. Famine. Not to mention imminent Armageddon. So. Happy! Happy! Happy! It certainly works for me.

'I take it you've got the rings,' I said.

'What rings?' said Dan. I laughed. Dan may have laughed too. Difficult to tell with that moustache.

We navigated University Avenue with its stray packs of students braying like hyenas, and soon we were strolling through Kelvinside Park. Only two and a half hours to go and we were still a good half mile from our goal. See? No drama, but who cares? It's a wedding. Let joy be unconfined. We passed the park café with its bright and lively come-hither look. A quick coffee or similar wouldn't go amiss at this stage, I mused. After all, we had the back of the journey broken. I was about to bring the subject up when Dan pointed to the play area.

'Kids,' he said. 'You and Blaise. Any plans on that front?'

I'd just begun to explain about the menopause[37] when a shrill scream cut across my reply. On the other side of the playground, a toddler, in trying to squeeze herself through the safety bar of a child's swing, had got her little neck stuck. A couple of mothers stood outside the perimeter railings having a cigarette break. Totally oblivious to the poor little mite. The child continued to scream. Heartrendingly. Dan and I, as one, sprang into action. Through the gate. Across the tarmac. Screeched to a halt.

'You lift,' panted Dan, 'I'll hold the swing.' Good plan, but the child wasn't to know that. Dan's moustache, up close, had no doubt further alarmed her. She raised the decibel level to twelve.

'Relax, little girl,' I soothed. 'We'll have you out of there in no time.' These reassuring words only succeeded in increasing the volume from the child. I tucked my hands under her flailing arms, at which point the young mothers paused in their cigarette break.

'Oi! You! FUCKIN PERV!'

That was one of them. Probably the biological one. She was still outside the perimeter fence but the sound carried. While I held and Dan tugged, she wheezed into the children's area, still clutching her cigarette. The

---

[37] Effects on female fertility of.

other woman was now on her mobile. The sound of the child's mother screaming at me from the cigarette-free section of her mouth, as she pummelled me round the head with tattooed fists, almost drowned out the wail of the approaching siren.

Funny how the police are always there when you don't need them. When we arrived at the station some twenty seven minutes later the desk sergeant gave me a quizzical look.

'Well now, Sir,' he said. 'You again.'

'We can explain everything,' Dan said, his moustache quivering with indignation.

'Besides,' I interrupted anxiously, 'it's not what it seems. I'm getting married in precisely one hour and forty eight minutes.'

He as good as chortled in my face. 'To a woman, Sir?' he said. 'I very much doubt that.'

'I don't much like your manner,' I said. I was, I freely admit, more than a bit agitated.

'I suspect your forthcoming nuptials may be the least of your worries, Sir,' said the desk sergeant genially. 'Perhaps you could accompany the arresting officer here into one of our interview rooms and we'll try to get to the bottom of this.'

'In that case,' I replied, with an uncanny sense of déjà vu, 'I think we're entitled to one free call.'

The desk sergeant plonked a phone on the counter and waved me on. 'In your own time, Sir,' he said. 'But I feel I must warn you, it's not looking good. Child abduction is a very serious offence. Added to which,' he moved closer for maximum effect, 'you do have previous.'

I glowered at him with malice aforethought.

'Last time,' I replied curtly, 'it was a baby, this time it's a child. Not the same thing at all. I might also point out, if you care to cast your mind back, that we were *returning* the baby, not *stealing* it.' I leaned on the counter for the coup de grace. 'My wife-to-be stole it.'

The desk sergeant was metaphorically floored. He had no comeback to *that*. But back to the present. Who to contact? I could hardly phone Blaise on this day of all days. Dan was the co-accused, so he was out, and I didn't keep a list of phone numbers in my head. Particularly for this sort of occasion, which always seemed to come as a surprise. I racked my brain, but for the life of me I could only remember one number. Blaise's mother's. I steeled myself and punched it in. The desk sergeant gave me the infuriatingly affable look. The look of the man who holds all the cards. Dan shifted uneasily. On the fifth ring Isobel answered.

'Isobel,' I bellowed, as cordially as I could under the circumstances. 'Dr. O'Shaughnessy here.' I'm neither a doctor nor an O'Shaughnessy, but try telling that to the formidable presence on the other end of the line. I braced myself. 'The thing is, I'm marrying your daughter in precisely,' I checked my watch, 'ninety seven minutes.'

'Indeed,' shouted Isobel over the roar of what sounded like an articulated lorry. Watching one of her beloved crime dramas, no doubt. Full volume.

'We were going to tell you,' I bellowed back, 'but decided to keep it as a surprise for the divorce.' Whoops. Blaise's little joke. It just slipped out. Nerves.

'Don't talk nonsense, young man,' roared Isobel.

'It's all over the social media.' I tried to say something mollifying, but you don't mollify a Presbyterian hewn from Cairngorm granite. 'Now I realise you're Irish, Doctor,' she shouted, 'so I'm trying to make allowances, but as far as the kirk is concerned that's bigamy.' She was referring to Blaise's first husband, whose name escapes me at present, but I didn't have time to go into that.

'Well, be that as it may,' I bellowed, 'the thing is, I'm being held at Her Majesty's Pleasure.'

'I'm not surprised,' roared Isobel. 'It's not only immoral. It's illegal.' I was happy to put her right on this little misunderstanding.

'You don't quite follow,' I bellowed. 'It's not for bigamy. It's for child abduction. You see – '

I could almost taste Isobel's disapproval on the other end of the line. 'Hmph. Does the arresting officer know you're Romish?'

'Aha,' I bellowed. 'I've got some excellent news on that front. Thanks to some correspondence with the Pope, not to mention the intercessions of a Jesuit, I'm delighted to say that I've reclaimed my soul and am now a free agent, unaffiliated, and independent of all religions, organised or other.' I almost said Amen, but fortunately Isobel was keen to interject.

'Once Romish, always Romish,' she shouted testily. 'Still, perhaps you'd better put the arresting officer on.'

'I can do better than that,' I bellowed. 'I can put you on to his immediate superior.' I gave the desk sergeant the thumbs up. He eyed me dolefully and took the phone.

'We'll come to bigamy later,' he said, then, to the phone, 'Good morning, ma'am.' Pause. 'He was seen lifting a screaming child off a swing.' Pause. 'Her mother was – ' Another pause, as he glanced at the arresting officer's notes. 'Apparently she was having a cigarette break outside the enclosure, but surely that's beside – ' Longer pause. 'Yes, ma'am. Modern parenting indeed. Having said that – ' Pause. 'Well in that case – ' Pause. 'I fully appreciate the extenuating circumstances, ma'am. I'll see to it directly. Now, not wishing to pry, but are you by any chance riding a motorcycle?' Pause. 'A mobility scooter. Silly me.' Pause. 'I'm not surprised, ma'am. Traffic-wise it's the busiest time of day. Might I suggest you try the hard shoulder. I'm sure you'll forgive me for saying this, but the use of a mobile phone on the M8 is strictly – ' Pause. 'Ah, that explains it. Bye now. Mind how you go.' The desk sergeant put the phone down. He shook as I had shaken when Isobel first entered my life. 'It's hands-free,' he said. 'Latest model.' He steadied himself at the counter. 'I've decided to discharge you on compassionate grounds,' he trembled. 'To be honest, I think you may have suffered enough.'

He seemed to rally slightly as we headed for the exit, no doubt relieved that Isobel belonged to my life, not his. 'Hold on a mo,' he said. He opened the door behind his desk. 'PC Clint,' he called. 'Little job for you. There's two gentlemen here late for a wedding up at Park Circus. Pop 'em round asap, will you? Cheers.' He turned back to the desk. 'Sorted, lads,' he said. 'You're free to leave without a stain on your characters.' He winked jovially, now fully recovered. 'Till the next time, eh?'

Short trip. Partick Police Station to Park Circus Registry Office. Seventy nine minutes to go. Top of the range cop car, complete with blue lights and sirens if required.

Young driver, keen to show his spurs. What could possibly go wrong? Well, Officer Clint for a start. He seemed troubled as he steered us out of the car park. As we joined a steady stream of traffic I caught him staring at me through the rear view mirror; as if he nursed some secret sorrow. I thought about breaking the silence and saying 'What is it, lad?' as we stopped at a set of traffic lights.

As the lights turned green Dan nudged me and leaned in close. 'He's taking us the wrong way,' he whispered. 'Will you tell him or will I?' I glanced at Clint. His fists were clenched on the wheel. His face was set. He stared straight ahead as if he wanted to be somewhere, anywhere, else. I was about to bring the subject up when Clint suddenly spoke.

'Thing is,' he said, 'it's my job to uphold the Law of the Land, and that includes gay marriage. Just so we're straight on that. My personal feelings don't come into it.'

Now that was quite the little speech. It seemed to come out of nowhere, but who can claim to fully understand what goes on in a policeman's head? I had my own deeply held views on gay marriage, but I really didn't think this was the time or place for that sort of discussion. I was about to point this out and suggest a quick about-turn when the car radio crackled into life. Domestic in Govan. Possibility of firearms. All available cars. Clint's face brightened and he sprang into action.

'I'm on it,' he roared over the screech of tyres, and before I could ask him to let us out and we'd walk the rest of the way thank you very much, he was off. Blue lights flashing. The works. We raced along Dumbarton Road and through the Clyde Tunnel. Clint roared the statistics on violent domestics at us over the wail of the siren. 'Not many gays yet. Course now they're getting married that'll be all change, no offence.'

'None taken,' said Dan as the car wailed out of the tunnel, traversed a mini-roundabout, swung left and screeched to a halt in front of a red sandstone tenement.

Clint flung the door open, which probably wasn't strictly necessary, and leapt out as if several lives depended on it. Three squad cars sat in a neat row with half a dozen officers chatting in a relaxed manner beside them. Moustaches. Peaked caps. At ease in their own uniforms. Crisis over, I would have thought, and sure enough, moments later Clint had switched from high action mode to bonding with his buddies. He put his foot on a fender, adjusted his stab vest, and stroked his neatly-clipped moustache. Here was a cop who wasn't going anywhere any time soon. I checked my watch and sighed a world-weary sigh.

Dan settled back in his seat. 'So what do you reckon about PC Clint?' he said.

'I'll tell you exactly what I reckon about PC Clint,' I said, trying to open the door. 'He'd never make it in the taxi business.'

Dan twinkled lugubriously. 'I think you know what I mean.'

'Never mind about that now,' I said. 'He's left the bloody child lock on.' I was about to ask Dan if he knew how to bloody drive one of these bloody cop cars when Clint sauntered back.

'Sorry about that,' he said, easing himself into his seat. 'Seems the little lady was firing blanks.' He adjusted his peaked helmet. 'Nice meeting the lads, though.' He put his hand on the ignition, then hesitated. 'Look,' he said. 'About this gay marriage thing. It's – ' he faltered. A stocky motorcycle cop strutted past the window, bulging from every orifice, and patted the top of the car. Clint raised his hand in a casual salute and sighed.

'It's what?' I said. I didn't particularly want to know, to be honest. I wanted to get moving. But it seemed to be one of those moments where you can't drive and talk at the same time. Clint gripped the wheel and wrestled with his demons for aeons. Probably ten seconds in real time. Eventually he was ready to share. 'It's my mum,' he said. 'She's – she's marrying – '

Words failed him. They failed me too. I had no idea where this was going. But Dan did. 'A woman?' he said helpfully. Clint bowed his head slowly and sank into his seat. 'Thought so,' whispered Dan. 'It ties in with the gay thing.'

I could see Clint's face in the rear view mirror. Scrunched up. Fighting back the tears. He looked about six. I patted his shoulder sympathetically. 'Mothers,' I said soothingly. 'They break a boy's heart.' He nodded in mournful agreement. I was beginning to think this could go on all day. How could I nip it in the bud before we all started talking about our feelings? 'Look at it this way, Clint,' I said. 'There comes a time when, face it, we have to let our mothers go. We've got to let them experience the world for themselves and yes, they're bound to make mistakes along the way or do things we don't necessarily like – '

'I know mine has,' said Dan.

' – but we've got to let them *go*, Clint,' I continued. 'Let them go to let them grow.' I squeezed his shoulder in a manly sort of way. 'Put it another way. She's left you to fend for yourself at the tender age of – how old *are* you, Clint?'

Clint sank further into his seat. 'Thirty two?'

'You see this as an attack on your masculinity, Clint. Am I right?' Clint may have squeaked a response or maybe it was the sound of his trousers rubbing against the seat as he tried to disappear altogether. 'Well I'm here to tell you it's nothing of the sort. So let's spin this towards the *positive*, Clint. Think of your mother as coming from a long line of inspirational women going out there and forging things anew.' I dredged up my list of inspirational women. 'Boudica.' At this point, to be honest, I stalled.

'Grace O'Malley,' added Dan helpfully. Possibly an old girlfriend. I let it pass and ran with the metaphorical ball.

'What about that Saudi suffragette who threw herself under the king's camels?' I was busking here, but Clint wasn't to know that. 'Embrace the shock of the new, Clint. I mean, answer me this. What harm is the poor woman doing? So she's marrying a woman. Live with it, man. I'll go further. Marry a woman yourself. It's all the rage. And while you're at it, try a bit of lateral thinking. You're not so much losing a mother as gaining – '

' – a mother,' said Dan, his eyes shining with what may have been tears.

'Now, what man in his right mind wouldn't sacrifice his trigger-pulling finger, not to mention six inches off his manhood' – I lowered my voice for maximum impact – 'to have two mammies!' I punched the back of his seat to drive the message home. 'You've hit the jackpot, man.

Vive la similarité !!!'

I stopped there. You can't top French. Silence fell, though I'm sure I heard a distinct snuffle from the driver's seat. Dan placed his hand on my knee and squeezed it gently. I could tell by the quivering of his moustache that he was deeply moved. Clint eventually stirred. He turned round in his seat. 'Two mums,' he said. 'That's beautiful, man. Thank you. Sincerely.' He blew his nose with genuine emotion and switched the siren back on. 'Right. What say we get you pair of love birds to the church on time?'

'Registry Office, Clint,' I corrected him. I didn't bother correcting him on the love birds reference, but as the car sped off I discreetly removed Dan's hand from my knee.

No sense inviting ridicule by arriving in a police car, so I got Clint to drop us at the bottom of the hill. Minutes later Dan and I were striding past the swing park for the second time. A child's ball plopped gently at my feet. Obviously a setup. I stepped pointedly over it and walked on.

Ahead of us loomed Park Circus.

'Enjoy your last few moments as a free man,' said Dan. 'Sure you want to go through with it?'

Did I? Time for a mental swither at this point? A bout of existential angst? I quickened my step. 'Just make sure you've got the rings,' I said.

'What rings?' said Dan.

I ignored him and marched briskly on. Dan's sense of humour tended to the juvenile and I was about to get married. Time to behave like a man.

Blaise looked radiant on the steps outside the registry office in her stunning African dress, a gift from legendary Senegalese author Treasure Mbotze. Radiant but troubled. I strode the last few feet and glanced at my watch. We were well on time. So what was the problem? Was it possible that Blaise herself was swithering?

'There's been a slight administrative hiccup,' she said, tears welling up in her voice. 'I'm afraid the 2pm slot is taken.'

'Taken?' I said. 'Of course it's taken. *We've* taken it. It was all sorted out months ago. I should know. I sorted it.' There was a slight pause. Blaise. Bonnie. Dan. They all paused together. A pregnant pause which contained, in its pregnancy, an implied criticism. But I wasn't having it. 'I booked it. It was confirmed,' I said. 'Hold on.' I took the registry office steps two at a time.

Bonnie ran after me. 'Dad.'

'Not now, Bonnie,' I said. 'Please.'

I pulled the door open and went in. The reception hall was magnificent, with its double staircase and high ceiling, its chandelier and triple windows. It was also full of people. Clint. Clint's mum and her partner, or possibly vice versa. Guests. An excited buzz of expectation. Bonnie tugged at my sleeve.

'There's a problem with the form, Dad.'

'There's always a problem with the form,' I said. 'Bloody bureaucracy.'

'No, Dad,' said Bonnie, her voice softer now. 'Bloody you. You put the wrong date.'

'No I didn't,' I said.

'Let me rephrase that,' said Bonnie. 'Right date, wrong year.'

I processed this information as Clint waved happily over. 'Did I?'

'Yes,' said Bonnie. 'You put next year.'

'Ah,' I said. 'Ah.' Our eyes met.[38] 'Could happen to anyone,' I said.

'No, Dad,' she sighed. 'Trust me. It couldn't.'

She was right. It couldn't. I waved back at Clint as he embraced his new mum. Bonnie took my arm and led me gently back to the door.

Blaise looked, for a moment, unbearably sad in the late autumn sunshine. I was standing beside her, trying to think of something to say, when Isobel appeared over the brow of the hill on what looked like a space age golf buggy, her goggles glinting in the sunlight, and Faye stepped, beaming, from a cab. Faye skipped gaily over.

'Where's the funeral?' she trilled. 'Don't tell me. Second thoughts. That's fine.' She put her arms round Blaise. 'Why mess with fate, right? You're doing great as you are.'

Blaise smiled, sweetly but sadly, which broke my guilty heart.

'I'm afraid there's been a bit of an administrative error,' she said.

All eyes were on me. Including Faye's. They knew. Faye knew. 'We – *I* booked for next year,' I said.

Faye poked me playfully in the ribs. 'Could happen to anyone,' she said. I may have looked less than convinced, but Faye continued beaming. 'Lighten up, guys,' she said. 'Come *on*, I mean what's a piece of paper? Besides, I'm a fully qualified celebrant.' She may have caught my look.

[38] Pregnantly.

'I know, I know,' she said. 'Nutritionist. Psychologist. Shen therapist. I teach Hatha Yoga, Judo up to level six and Book Binding. I also play tenor saxophone in *The Clits* but don't tell my mother. Plus I'm a fully qualified accountant, chartered. My card. All this and chronic fatigue syndrome! So why not celebrant, I thought. I qualified yesterday.' She looked at her watch. 'Busy busy busy, but I think I can just about slot you in.'

Delusional? Possibly, but Faye had injected a much needed shot of lunatic energy into proceedings, and suddenly all was harmony and joy. Minutes later we stood on a grassy knoll overlooking the River Kelvin. Blaise, Faye, Bonnie. Isobel, Dan and me.

I won't dwell on the ceremony. Faye's fertility dance was strictly symbolic, apparently – it referred to *creative* fertility – but it drew a sizeable crowd, and a couple of bookings for future gigs, as she put it. Her references to being at one with the oneness, and suchlike, were not to my taste, although Dan lapped it all up with missionary zeal. Possible romance there? They were certainly the right height for each other. Isobel, for her part, may have voted with her ears. Her hearing aid lay unused in her lap. We made eye contact under her goggles, and I was struck by a curious thought. Father Tristan the Jesuit. Tristan and Isolde. Could that gentle cleric, lovelorn all these years, have said, not Tristan and Isolde, but Tristan and Isobel? Isobel's eyes told me nothing, but she surveyed proceedings with what may have been a Presbyterian smile softening the impenetrable, hewn-granite contours of her face. Who knew what torrid secrets lurked thereunder?

I was overcome with the male equivalent of emotion.

'Dan,' I cried joyfully. 'The rings.'

'What rings?' said Dan.

Bonnie exchanged a female-bonding-type look with Blaise, opened her shoulder bag, and produced two rings from its mysterious, female depths.

'*These* rings,' she said.

I thanked Bonnie, took the smaller of the two in one hand, and Blaise's hand in the other. The sun shone behind her as it was fated to do since the dawn of time. It would explode with joy at some indeterminate point in the future at the memory of this beautiful moment, but first there was the small matter of forever.

Bonus Stories

Prune Surprise

I was opening that night at the Edinburgh Festival. My new one-man show. The tension at my flat was almost unbearable.

'Sorry?' I said. 'Could you repeat that?'

Suzette, or *la Directrice* as she called herself, uncurled slightly on the sofa.

'Ze three aunts,' she purred, ''ave got to go. Zey're not believable.'

'No no,' I hissed. '*You're* not believable. The show goes up in four hours, and besides,' I prodded my finger at her cigarette smoke, 'they actually exist. In fact, I almost wish they were here now so I could prove the point.'

The doorbell rang.

'Ah. Zat will be zem now.'

I laughed nervously. Edinburgh at festival time was once described as 'the Gomorrah of the north'. Gomorrah sued and won. Inference? It was no place for three genteel ladies approaching the century mark. Besides, I couldn't possibly let them anywhere near my show. It mentioned condoms – uncritically – and used the word bloody. Twice.

But there's no way it could be them. Suzette was being – how you say? – humorous. Knowing my aunts, they were probably on their knees in some dimly lit Dublin church weeping and gnashing their gums. Atoning, the God-fearing little sweeties, for a blameless life. I opened the door.

The postman.

Well *that* was a relief. Suzette is not a woman to whip out in front of the sainted aunts. I don't think I'm giving too much away to say that she's slept with every member of the cast.

I was about to broach this delicate subject when the doorbell rang again.

'Ah hello, Een.'

'Surprise surprise.'

'Guess who?'

That, by the way, was all three of them.

I rushed back into the living room. Rude? Perhaps, but this was serious.

'Out, Suzette. Now. I'll explain later.'

'Commong?'

A very French response, but I was having none of it. 'My maiden aunts are here. I can't possibly introduce them to a woman like you. You've slept with every member of the cast.'

'But Yann. It's a one-man show.'

'I was referring to last year's production of *Les Miserables* in Croydon.'

By the time I'd steered Suzette out of the living room my aunts had managed to shuffle more than half way along the hall.

'There you are, Een.'

'Playing hide and seek on your old aunties.'

'And who's the lovely lady?'

'My cleaning lady. Suzette. She's French, so I'm afraid small talk is quite out of the question. Just wave.'

Suzette, I'm afraid, insisted on being unnecessarily Gallic at this point.

'Cleaning lady? Moi?'

'Don't knock it,' I said. 'It's the third oldest profession. Arrividerci.' And then, with a nod to Camus, 'Don't be a stranger.'

'One momong,' she said. 'I must not forget my 'euveur.'

''euveur?'

'My 'euveur. With which I 'euveur the carpette in my capacité as your cleaning lady.'

The woman had obviously flipped. I gave her the Hoover, and soon all that remained of her was a cloud of cigarette smoke, several items of French underwear and the odd beret.

Five minutes later I was busy organizing my aunts.

'Now listen, ladies', I said. 'You're here for an overnight stay. That much is clear. You came over on a tacky airline – '

'Tree for the price of one, Een.'

'Bring your own goggles.'

'Kindly don't interrupt. You forgot to collect your luggage at the airport. Dotage. There's no shame in it.'

'But Een – '

'Aren't we forgetting something?' They fell silent. '*That's* better. Now the fact of the matter, ladies, is that you're innocents abroad. You need looking after. So. Have you ever been to Edinburgh before?'

'God yes, Een. Nineteen tirty six.'

'Excellent,' I said. 'It hasn't changed a bit.'

I was lying, of course, but I had to keep them away from the decadence of the festival and, more importantly, my show.

'Come,' I said with old world courtesy. 'let me show

you an educational time.'

'*Aw, we were going to see the sights, Een.*'

'*On an open neck bus.*'

'Too dangerous, ladies. Low bridges and the like. Your hats would never survive it. Let's go.'

I knew exactly what I had in mind. Old Edinburgh. The older the better. And what could be older than the ancient, venerable Church of the Holy Rude? It had the benefit of being local, so I hurried them out the door. Down the wynd. Past the skip with my Hoover resting on top. Under the 'Blisit be God for al his giftis' sign.

My aunts were transfixed. Such history. Such graves.

'*It's beautiful, Een. Wouldn't it be lovely to be dead, though.*'

'*So romantic. We should be dead years ago.*'

'*I tink we left it too late, Een. It'll probably never happen now.*'

They were wittering on like this as women of a certain age are wont to do when a man of God strode towards us. Gaunt. Piercing stare. Shock of white eyebrows. They were sure to put their feet in it. Father instead of Pastor. Or is it Reverend? Or Moderator? Anyway, that sort of thing.

He towered over us with the pained look of a man wearing barbed wire underpants.

'*Ah, hello Father.*[39]'

'*We were just saying wouldn't it be lovely to be dead.*'

Ah. They'd obviously picked his speciality subject. His face softened, and within minutes he was offering them a conducted tour of the dungeons.

This suited my plans admirably. I needed time alone.

---

[39] See?

Opening night was imminent and I was still a bit rusty on the script front. I decided on a quick run through there and then. Discreetly, of course; I trod on sanctified ground. But I may have got slightly carried away in the three-maiden-aunts-get-nostalgic scene.

'Ahhh. Will you look at him in this one when he was two.'
'With his little rosy cheeks.'
'On his little rosy botty.'
'Coo-eee!'

Coo-ee? Odd. That wasn't in the show.

'We're back, Een!'

Aah. I awoke as from a reverie. The explanation was simple. They were back.

'He says this is venue four tree two, Een.
'Venue four tree two. That's very high, isn't it?'
'Isn't that great though, Een. Venue four tree two.'

Venue four three two. Oh my God. The church was part of the festival. Is nothing sacred any more? I quickly changed the subject to the distinguished sons of Edinburgh interred beneath our feet. City worthies. Elders. Burghers.

'Speaking of which, Een, I could eat a horse.'
'So could I, Een.'
'Me too. Is there a race track near?'

They giggled uproariously, but I stilled them with a look.

'Ladies,' I admonished. 'Desist. Forthwith. We tread on hallowed ground.'

But they had a point. Food. Under normal circumstances I would have made them my celebrated brown rice risotto with prune surprise.

There was no time for cordon bleu, however, so we

went to the local chip shop. Not my style, but quick. Or at least it would have been if the staff had used subtitles.

'Salt 'n' sauce?'

'Pardon?'

'Salt 'n' sauce?'

'I'm terribly sorry. I can't – '

'Easy on the salt but lashin's of sauce, tanks. We're on hollyers.'

'And pudding. Pudding pudding we want pudding. Pudding pudding we want – '

'Stop!' I commanded. 'Just tell the nice man what you're having.'

'I tink we'll go for the healty option, Een. Maltesers in batter.'

Twenty minutes later they were flicking maltesers across the living room while I busied myself planning their evening. I had to leave for the show in half an hour and I couldn't risk them roaming the streets on their own. Battered maltesers bounced off my head as I tried to rack what was left of my brain. What to do? What to – Aha!

'Bedtime, girls! Chop chop!'

Now I don't know what it is about women, but Suzette had spent two blissful nights in my company – just the two, as my diary erotically attests – and yet the place was littered with nighties. French nighties, it has to be said, but a nightie's a nightie for a' that. So I made them cocoa, shooed them into their frillies and tucked them in.

'Story, Een.'

'We want a story. We want a story. We want – '

'All right. All right. As long as you promise to go to sleep directly afterwards.'

'We-e-e-e – promise.'

Actually, a story was probably a good idea, come to think of it. Psychologically speaking. They wouldn't go a-wandering after *this* one.

'Once upon a time,' I began, my stentorian voice rebounding off the walls like maltesers in batter, 'there were three very naughty girls.'

'We don't say naughty in Dublin, Een.'
'We say bold.'
'All right then. Three bold girls.'
'Of course bold could mean brave, Een.'
'Were they brave, Een? Were they?'
'No. They were naughty bold. Now settle down.'

It was a particularly gruesome story involving the wynds of nineteenth century Edinburgh, the haar in from the north sea and a psychotic doctor with five o'clock shadow on his palms. My aunts quaked in their little French numbers. After the inevitable bloodbath I pecked them goodnight, closed the bedroom door quietly and prepared myself for the off. No sense in taking chances, I thought, so on my way out, and strictly as a precautionary measure, I hid their hats.

Now I am not a vain man – quite the opposite, in fact – and if I seem to be the subject of fawning adulation as this modest tale unfolds I can only plead the artist's humble excuse. The plot demands it.

The show went well. Enough of that. I was taking a twelfth curtain call – a feat in itself as there was no curtain – when a leading reviewer from Scotland's most influential daily stood up.

'I have a confession to make,' he announced. 'Some years back I wrote that this man, this veritable Adonis of a man with his husky voice and chiselled masculinity, was too sexually alluring to be a truly great comedian. Well, I'm here to tell you I was wrong. Ian...' The voice at this point became tremulous and pleading. 'I want to share your bed.'

Quite an admission. I was momentarily thrown, but my innate breeding and old-fashioned good manners came to the rescue.

'It's a very kind offer,' I said, 'but the bed is full up already. Three women. French nighties. Doubt if I'll get in there myself tonight, frankly.'

Problem solved, you might be forgiven for thinking. Hugs all round. Not so. His beard turned red with fury.

'I've closed them in bigger dumps than *this*, sweetie.'

Worse was to follow. I made the mistake of leaving the venue. He pounced. There were fisticuffs. Twelve cameras clicked at once. Catastrophe! What if the story appeared on the front page of his salubrious daily? My aunts would be sure to spot it. All would be revealed. I was distraught.

I paced the city waiting for the first edition. The haar was in from the sea. My GP rushed past with a bloodstained mouth. The night air was filled with casual obscenities. Minor Scottish novelists rushed around taking notes. I paced outside the offices of the city desk until, at last, the first edition was disgorged.

I almost mangled the poor lad's bicycle in my eagerness to get hold of a copy. I scoured the front page but I needn't have worried. 'Queen Mother Still Dead.'

I began to relax a bit. Perhaps I'd been a tad jittery. The photographers, on mature reflection, had all been Japanese. Having said that, I needed a drink. Something a bit stronger than cocoa; so I dropped by the Festival Club. The joint was *jump*ing.

In the corner, fondling a Ricard, sensual, androgynous, louche, lounged Suzette. We'd make love later, but first there was the small matter of the Hoover. I elbowed my way over. She was deep in conversation with… what the hell were my maiden aunts doing in berets?

'In the looks department now, Suzette, we wouldn't have Sartre down as France's finest hour.'

'But what a lover.'

'Speaking of lovers, Suzette, here's yours.'

'Howaya, Een. Mine's a Pernod.'

'And by the way, we caught your show.'

'You've certainly got something to work on.'

'But for God's sake drop the tree oul wans, Een.'

'Sure no one's like that in real life.'

The Nut House

I had just placed the job advertisement in the window and was chopping ingredients for the day's special when the phone rang.

'Nut House?' I said. 'No, no. It's a common mistake, Doctor. This is the vegetarian restaurant of the same name.'

No sooner had I put the phone down and got back to work than the door burst open and in burst a man with a gun. That's two bursts in one sentence, but the word has a certain onomatopoeic quality and it suited both door and man. So. Door. Man with gun. Double burst.

He pointed the gun at me in what I can only describe as an aggressive manner.

'Put the knife down,' he spat. 'And move away from the courgette. Now.'

My restaurant my rules I thought, but there was something in his tone which wouldn't be gainsaid. I did as he asked.

'If this is about the job,' I said, 'then I have to tell you you've got off to a very bad start. Look at those shoes. Filthy.'

'It's not about the job.'

'In that case,' I said, wiping my hands on my apron, 'what can I get you?'

I sincerely hoped he wasn't going to say 'Mmmn. Your special looks nice. Think I'll plump for that.' I have an unfortunate habit of chalking up the menu first, then getting down to the more protracted business of preparing and cooking. Call it aggressive marketing. At any rate, there it stood. 'Today's Special – Pizza Del Journo.'

'I'm not hungry,' he snapped. Still, I noted, brandishing the gun.

'Café Latte?' I said. 'Cappuccino? Americano? Espresso? Café Del Journo?'

I was starting to feel flamboyant in a Mediterranean sort of way, but he didn't seem impressed. His attention had been diverted by the sudden arrival of a veritable phalanx of cop cars in the street outside. Sirens blaring. Tyres squealing. Horns tooting. And encroaching on the cycle lane with apparent impunity. I was, however, pretty sanguine about the whole thing. This is the world we live in. Accept it or look elsewhere. My new acquaintance, on the other hand, was positively *vexed*.

'Jesus!'

He threw a table over – not, fortunately, one I'd already laid – crouched behind it and waggled his pistol. A tad provocative to my way of thinking, but I had other things to worry about. Not a single enquiry since I'd placed the job ad. I mean what is it with kids these days? Do they not *want* to work? I was also feeling a bit sensitive about the apparent lack of custom. Time, perhaps, to have a rethink on the price structure. As if that wasn't enough, I was still at the chopping, dicing, grating stage, when I should be simmering at the very least. My uninvited guest may have been above such mundane matters, but I had a business to run.

'Mind if I get on?' I said. And then, pointedly, 'I mean these dishes don't cook themselves.'

He seemed preoccupied with his own thoughts, so I

took that as a yes. And as I diced the carrots, chopped the leeks and grated the Parmesan, I studied the back of his head. Orange bristles stood out from his neck like quills upon the fretful porpentine. The tension in his shoulder muscles was palpable. Now I don't wish to be melodramatic, but he really did look capable of inflicting serious injury on person or persons unknown. Diet, I thought. Too much raw meat. This is a typical vegetarian response, but it's a well known fact: non-carnivores are far less likely to respond aggressively in any given situation; Hitler being the honourable exception to this particular rule.

And then it struck me. This aggression had nothing to *do* with diet. But of course! How could I have been so blind? Orange hair? Accent not a million miles from the Catholic quarter of Ballymena? I knew Ballymena well, having been drummed out of there on several occasions. Failure to wear bowler hat in public place. Accent likely to cause breach of peace. That sort of thing. But there I had it. The key to all his pent up fury. His incandescent rage. And before I could stop myself I blurted my thoughts into words. 'For pity's sake put the gun down, lad. You're in Edinburgh now. And besides, the blessed war is over.'

Well that was a great relief. Momentarily.

'What the hell are you on about?' he all but shrieked. And then he got back to his ridiculous game with the police. One of whom was bellowing into a megaphone in a shocking display of inconsideration. Noise pollution? Karaoke by the back door *I* call it.

But I digress.

'Oh yes,' I said. 'The war ended some time back.

Catholics and Protestants now live together in peace and harmony. Apart, obviously, from the odd ritual slaughter.'

The back of his head gave me a withering look.

'It's nothing to do with the war,' he snapped.

I was more than happy to correct him on this particular point.

'Ah, but that's where you're wrong, you see. It's a post traumatic stress type thing. The psychological inability to let seven hundred years of mindless brutality go. And you've got it, sonny. In spades.'

He said nothing. A helicopter was about to land on the roof opposite and it may have appealed to his boyish sense of wonder. At any rate he was transfixed by it's perilous descent. But I was on a roll, so I sculpted a yam into peace symbols and developed my thesis anyway.

'Oh, we've all experienced the after effects of conflict,' I said. 'Take my tragic background, for instance. Clontarf. A seemingly innocuous north Dublin suburb where the rich coexist in apparent peace with the even richer. And yet' – my voice here rose with the still raw emotion – 'Brian Boru, High King of All Ireland, was savagely murdered there as he lay relaxing in his tent. Admittedly this happened a long time ago – 1014 to be precise – but it still has the power to shock.'

I whittled a marrow into the shape of a medieval axe – a symptom, perhaps, of my inner turmoil – and wiped away a tear or two of rage.

'Your point?' snapped my solitary customer.

'My point,' I said, gently and not without love, 'is that wounds heal slowly. So put the gun down. Have a tossed salad on the house.' I dropped my voice to a truth and reconciliation whisper. 'Let it go.'

The back of his head clenched with rage.

'You have no idea, have you?' he trembled. 'No idea.'

I was about to take issue with him when I saw that his attention had flitted elsewhere. It was now taken up with a row of marksmen lining the roof opposite. I failed to see the attraction - possibly a boy thing - but he was *riveted*.

He crouched further behind the table and marinated in his own sweat.

'Okay, big man,' he said. 'Here's the deal. We're in for the long haul. So get on that phone and order a takeaway pizza.'

'But – '

'Just do it.'

'I was about to say,' I replied curtly, 'that this is a world renowned outlet for superior pizza. What can I get you?'

He turned menacingly towards me, his little red face puckered up in fury.

'One takeaway pizza,' he intoned. 'Delivered by a spotty youth on a Lambretta. In a cardboard box.'

I pouted involuntarily.

'Well I'm not acceding to your heinous demands,' I said. 'And that's final.'

He cocked his pistol.

'Final? Are you absolutely sure about that?'

'Oh yes,' I said. 'So go on. You can kill *me*, that's the easy bit. But know this. There will always be others to carry on the tradition of culinary excellence.'

I hadn't intended this as an appeal to his better nature – he was, after all, a cardboard box man – but for some reason it had the desired effect. He sighed and lowered the gun.

'Okay,' he said. 'Forget the pizza. Just get on the blower and phone a sympathetic journalist. Then bring the phone over here. A free and frank interview. My voice *will* be heard.'

'Slight problem there,' I said. 'I only know one journalist and...'

'Call him,' he snapped, recocking his pistol and snarling for added effect.

'Could be a her,' I said, flaunting my feminist credentials.

'Her then.'

'But he's a him.'

Point made, I dialled the number.

'Michel?' I said. 'There's...'

'Pass it over.' He was still snarling. 'And no funny business.'

I lifted the phone, moved slowly towards him and passed it gingerly over. He grabbed the receiver.

'Listen up,' he said. 'I've just shot a traffic warden.'

Interesting development, this. I genuinely hadn't been expecting it. He paused. And then he was off again.

'What do you mean what's it got to do with you? You're a journalist. It's a scoop. So get typing and keep your mouth to yourself. Okay. Ready?'

He paused again, went slowly purple, and slammed the phone down.

'Not interested?' he screamed. 'Not interested? What sort of crap is that? I've just shot a man to death and he's not interested? I mean, I mean, what sort of idiot *is* this?"

'I did try to tell you,' I admonished gently. 'He's the restaurant critic.'

He lowered his gun and sighed a heart-rending sigh.

'Hey, come on,' I said. '*I'm* interested. Tell *me*.'

He sighed again.

'But I need to tell the *world*,' he said.

'No problem,' I said. 'I'll pass it on.' He seemed resistant. 'Word of mouth,' I said. 'Don't knock it.'

'Okay,' he said. 'I got a parking ticket. I snapped. I shot the warden.'

I snorted with ill-concealed derision.

'Is that all? I mean, good God, man. The world is full of traffic wardens. But there's something else, isn't there?' He was trembling openly now.

'I was just standing in the road,' he sobbed. 'So he gave me a ticket. I mean, I don't even *drive*.'

I placed a sympathetic hand a discreet distance from his shoulder.

'There there,' I said. 'There there there.' I moved slightly closer. 'But there's something *else*, isn't there? Something deeper?' I urged in my best you-may-have-murdered-several-hundred-people-in-the-past-but-hey-let's-look-to-the-future manner. 'You haven't told me everything.'

He was sobbing openly now.

'After the ceasefire,' he wept, 'I was out of a job. There just wasn't any call for, well, you know. So I thought, new start, change of scenery, move country. Apply to retrain as traffic warden.' He paused to weep afresh. 'But they wouldn't have me.'

'I know I know,' I soothed. 'No Catholics need apply.'

'It wasn't that,' he wailed. 'It's – It's – ' He paused to collect his thoughts. 'I couldn't grow a moustache.'

'Sorry?'

'Have you ever seen a traffic warden without a moustache?'

I thought about it for a moment.

'What about lady traffic wardens?'

'No exceptions.'

As he crouched there trembling and weeping I examined the soft flesh-coloured down on his upper lip. And I suddenly understood. He'd been humiliated. Made to feel inadequate. Powerless. And just then, as if to prove the point, a couple of dozen paratroopers stormed in through the window and took his gun away.

As he lay pinned to the floor I was struck by a serendipitous thought. I hadn't had a single enquiry about that job ad. I'd given it full prominence on the window display and yet no-one had bothered to apply.

But maybe here was an opportunity. As my gun-toting friend lay trussed up on the floor like an oven ready nut roast, I finally felt able to place that hand on his shoulder.

'Look,' I said gently, reassuringly. 'Forget about those nasty traffic wardens. So what if they laughed at you and made you feel less than a man. It's an old and well-tested emasculation technique. But hey, maybe it's time to move on.'

I picked the job ad off the floor where it rested on shards of glass, crumpled it and tossed it aside.

'I don't think we need to interview anyone else,' I said. 'There's a job for you here if you want it. You have a certain way with a table. Not to mention a pleasing manner when you manage to calm yourself down.'

I moved in closer and smoothed his savage brow.

'Waitressing,' I ventured. 'Fancy giving it a whirl?'

Round Ireland With An Inanimate Household Object

It all started with a wager. I was living in London at the time, and a friend bet me I wouldn't hitchhike round Ireland with an inanimate household object. He was right. I wouldn't. Later that evening he lured me into a public house, plied me with drink, and repeated the bet. Apparently.

The following morning I awoke with a pounding headache and a ringing in my ears. I picked up the phone.

'Listen, I've hired a Luton van for the trip to Holyhead. I mean, we can't expect you to do the British isles as well.'

I was stunned. Luton van? Holyhead? Then it all came back to me. The camaraderie. The banter. The incident with the policeman's helmet. And this time, spurred on by a large crowd of well-wishers, I'd accepted the bet.

There was no way out. I had to do it.

I spent the following hours in a state of mounting gloom. Yet as the day progressed the idea began to have a certain appeal. My career as the finest flowering of a generation of light entertainers was floundering somewhat. This could be the very thing to get it moving. I began to inhale the heady whiff of publicity. The camera crews, chat show hosts and serious social commentators queueing up to swell the ranks of this wildly comic odyssey. Not to mention the best-selling book. Round Ireland With A –

The question was, which particular inanimate household object? It had to be something worthy of such an undertaking. Eyecatching. Humorous. Capable of uniting the whole country in an orgy of glee. I looked around the flat and discarded several ideas on the grounds of size. Round Ireland With A Spoon, for instance. You could just slip a spoon into the nearest available pocket. Result? You'd look exactly the same as someone who wasn't carrying a spoon. An exercise of almost existential pointlessness.

I decided to make a list of larger objects and wandered round the flat with a notebook doing just that.

Dustpan and brush. Hoover. Stair carpet. Indoor herb garden. Ornamental grandfather clock. Removable double glazing. Nothing to fire the blood there. I was about to repair to the slough of despond when inspiration struck. The inanimate household object didn't have to come from my flat. Of course. Within seconds of this blinding insight I had settled on the object in question: My aged parents' marital four poster bed. I phoned my friend in a state of no small excitement.

He put it to me that this might prove inconvenient.

'Not at all,' I replied. 'They're octogenarians. They probably won't even notice.'

My aged parents lived, at the time, in a south London suburb in sheltered accommodation. We drove the Luton van round later that night.

I won't dwell on the difficulty of getting the bed downstairs, but our efforts were somewhat hampered by the width of the stairs and our mutual desire not to rouse my parents from their fitful slumbers. They eventually woke up just as we were passing through Bangor. We were alerted to this state of affairs by a furious banging in the heart of the van. We pulled over, unlocked the back door and out they staggered, blinking, onto the grass verge. Expressing the hope that they had remembered to bring their free bus passes we clambered back in and sped towards the waiting boat.

Once aboard I waved my old and trusted friend goodbye as I set out, complete with bed, on my historic voyage. The other passengers paid me no heed, possibly of the opinion that I couldn't afford a berth for the night. Ah well. I got a passing sailor to tuck me in on the main deck and thought no more about it.

But Dublin? I fully expected the publicity circus to start rolling in this bustling metropolis. Not so. I decided to alert press and media to my hilarious project, but the response was the same from all quarters.

'I think we'll pass on that one,' they said. Aha, I thought. The shock of the new. Their loss.

As for the inhabitants of Ireland's present capital, they appeared, if such a thing were possible, not to notice me! As I traversed the city, castors squeaking, candlewick bedspread billowing in the early morning gale, the heavily populated main thoroughfare seemed paralyzed by indifference. No ballads to be written in my honour here, I fancied.

I pressed on till I hit the main road south, parked the bed on the inside lane and stuck out a tentative thumb. Now Ireland is a small country compared to, say, a much larger country. Such things are relative, but it seemed to grow in scale as the prospect of a lift got more and more remote. Perhaps I had been overambitious. The average family saloon is hardly equipped to accommodate a four poster bed, marital or otherwise, on the back seat. A single bed might have suited my purposes better. Better still, a sleeping bag with groundsheet. But where's the comedy in that?

I was mulling this over when a removals van, speeding in the other direction, executed a u-turn and parked, with a spray of water and a screech of brakes, directly in front of the bed. The driver jumped out.

'Where to?' he said, hoisting the bed into the back.

'Newtownmountkennedy,' I cried, jumping into the passenger seat.

Excellent, I thought. My luck had changed. And yet, in spite of his charitable gesture, the driver seemed a morose individual. He careered along without a word and my cheerful account of my proposed trip was met with frowning indifference. We reached our destination within the hour and he hoisted the bed back out.

'That will be €47.32,' he quipped.

I laughed heartily at his merry jest but stopped when he added VAT.

I soon put that little episode behind me but felt, as I inched my way slowly south, that I wasn't getting anywhere in my quest to engage the public. So I decided to drop into a local hostelry, and just about managed to squeeze the four-poster through the front entrance.

'Greetings,' I panted merrily. 'I've come in search of the crack. The wild beat of the bodhrán, the mournful sound of the pipes. The songs. The stories. The Joycean quote in casual conversation. The Guinness.' I was about to add the hundred thousand welcomes and the blarney but my heart wasn't in it. Through a thick fug of smoke I noticed a handful of sad-eyed refugees huddled round the television watching an Australian soap.

The barman gave me a lugubrious look.

'We'll buy the book.'

He gave me another lugubrious look and went back to the soap. I heaved the bed back outside and pressed onward with fresh purpose. I felt refreshed. Invigorated. No publicity. No media circus. And yet the barman of this small and seemingly insignificant pub had actually mentioned my forthcoming book. How could this be? Not only that. He - they! - were going to buy it. I was momentarily ecstatic.

And then, at the foot of a particularly steep incline, I noticed something which put an entirely different perspective on matters. Not twenty yards in front an upright piano of the type favoured by people christened Fats was inching its way forward. And behind it, straining and gasping and rolling a cigarette with her free hand, loomed a comedienne of my acquaintance.

I was stunned. This was the last thing I'd expected. I pondered the implications. A working holiday, perhaps? Booked to accompany herself at a small village in Cork but unable to afford the transport? It seemed unlikely. Fearing the worst I redoubled my efforts and was soon panting alongside her just below the brow of the hill.

'Oh, this old thing,' she wheezed. 'I woke up with a stinking hangover yesterday and wouldn't you just know it. I'd made a stupid drunken bet. Then I thought, hold on, there's a best-selling book in this. So what are you up to yourself these days?'

'Oh, this and that,' I grimaced with a sinking heart. 'Well, must get on.' I waved her a cheerless goodbye and strained on to the brow of the hill.

I wiped my own brow and tried to admire the view. There before me, in all its panoramic splendour, lay the broad sweep of the valley below. The verdant fields. The far-off hills. Not undulating, perhaps, but close to it. And, dotted along the way a veritable depression of comedians careering towards the Mitchelstown bypass; each of them pushing, pulling or clutching an inanimate household object. I narrowed my eyes and gazed into the distance. Round Ireland With A Hostess Trolley; A Tumble Drier; A Large Bowl Of Ornamental Fruit. A pertinent fact had to be faced: The publishing world could only take so much.

Then the removals van roared past. Beside the driver sat yet another comedian fondling yet another inanimate household object. That clinched it. Round Ireland With A Corby Trouser Press. How could anyone hope to follow that?

I was reflecting on this most profound of questions when I noticed that the inhabitants of a nearby car park were all studiously ignoring me. Embarrassment? Pity? Whatever the motive I began to feel exceedingly foolish. I tried to look as if a man standing on the brow of a hill with his parents' marital four poster bed was the most natural thing in the world. It wasn't. I tried to pretend the bed was an oddly shaped yet highly intriguing vintage car in urgent need of an overhaul. I began to whistle tunelessly like a mechanic in a bad film. I checked the castors for signs of wear; the candlewick bedspread for mould; I even turned my father's pillow over to hide the brylcreem stain. But not everyone, I sensed, was fooled.

I was about to press on with a weary sigh when a small

child broke ranks and ran towards me. A small child, yes, but full, no doubt, of kind thoughts and balming words. I can see her still, her golden ringlets kissed by the sun and caressed by the early evening breeze as she opened her mouth to speak.

'Deirdre,' cried her father. 'What have I told you about talking to losers. That's no way to get on.' And then he turned his attention to me. 'If you're going to do something crazy, pal, then take my advice: Be first. I mean, for God's sake,' he continued, 'who remembers the second guy up Everest?'

He was right, of course. Enough said. I shrugged, turned the four-poster round and wearily retraced my steps. I was still some miles from Newtownmountkennedy when the removals van pulled up and offered me a 50% reduction as a regular customer. But I was on my own private Calvary at this stage and ploughed on, alone and unloved.

Shortly afterwards I passed a female triple act of my acquaintance coming the other way. With a three-piece suite.

'Don't mind us askin',' they said. 'What gives with the bed?'

'Oh, that,' I said. 'I'm delivering it to my parents in south London.'

'Right. Gotcha. Bye now.' And I could hear their ribald laughter taunting me for several miles down the road.

After that it was Dublin. The sea. The Luton van. And some days later, abject and humiliated, I squeezed the four-poster through my parents front door in mounting gloom. Past a phalanx of cameras. Reporters.

Casual onlookers.

Mother was signing a document in the living room, overseen by a young man with leather trousers and cash register eyes. She gave me a cheery wave as I negotiated the first flight of stairs.

'Come in here a sec, son. I've just hit the jackpot.'

I plonked the bed on the landing and made my way, with an ever sinking heart, downstairs. Mother thrust the document into my hand with undisguised joy.

'From Bangor to Penge in a Bri-Nylon Nightie,' she beamed. 'This nice young man seems to think there's a book in it.'

Acknowledgements

Salmon Chamareemo was published in New Writing Scotland 27.

A Brisk Hike Up The Trossachs was published in Northwords Now.

Bottled Air was published in New Escapologist.

Soggy Bottom Baby was published in Gutter Magazine 12 , Spring 2015.

Salmon Chamareemo and *Prune Surprise* were both recorded live by the author at the Edinburgh Festival as part of *Comic Fringes* for BBC Radio 4.

The Nut House was read by the author and broadcast on BBC Radio 4.

The following were read by the author and broadcast as the story series *'Bottled Air'* on BBC Radio 4: *Bottled Air, A Brisk Hike Up The Trossachs, War and the Menopause, Soggy Bottom Baby* and *Death of a Ladles Man*.

Ian Macpherson

Ian Macpherson is a comedian and writer from Dublin. He won the first Time Out London Comedy Award in 1988 and has written and performed several one-man shows at the Edinburgh Festival. His first novel *Deep Probings: The Autobiography of Ireland's Greatest Living Genius* was broadcast on Radio 4's Book at Bedtime. He has had several plays produced both for stage and radio. A recipient of the Robert Louis Stevenson Writing Prize, he has written several books for children. When not appearing at book and literary festivals he lives in Glasgow's West End with poet Magi Gibson, his many awards, and a suitcase full of memories.

'Pre-dating and pre-empting all contemporary Irish comics, and the originator of the most influential joke of all time, Ian Macpherson is the Newgrange Megalithic Passage Tomb of stand-up comedy'

STEWART LEE

'The Comedians' Comedian'

IRISH TIMES

'Ian was one of the first stand ups I ever saw live, and I longed for gags like his'

HARRY HILL

'One of the most creative and intelligent comedians I've ever seen'

GUARDIAN

'For a funny Celt, catch tonight's last episode of the current Book at Bedtime - BBC Radio 4. The memoirs of Fiachra MacFiach, read with perfect gravity by Ian Macpherson, reveal a sort of Irish Pooter'

THE FINANCIAL TIMES

'Comedy's answer to James Joyce'

ARTHUR SMITH – BBC RADIO 4

'DisComBoBuLatE – with host Ian Macpherson – delivered a brilliant, thought-provoking and highly entertaining mix of literature and comedy at the Edinburgh International Book Festival. It was one of the popular hits of the festival and also one of my own personal highlights'

NICK BARLEY – DIRECTOR –
EDINBURGH INTERNATIONAL BOOK FESTIVAL